COWBOY JUDGMENT

USA TODAY BESTSELLING AUTHOR

BARB HAN

TORJAKE PUBLISHING

Editing: Ali Williams

Cover Design: Jacob's Cover Designs

Proofreading: Judicious Revisions

To my family for unwavering love and support. I can't imagine doing life with anyone else. I love you guys with all my heart.

CONTENTS

Kurt Johnson stared at the newspaper sprawled across his kitchen table. He took another lap around the small, craftsman-style house as stress pulled his shoulder muscles taut. He flexed and released his fingers a few times in an attempt to work off the tension building. Rolling his head from side-to-side didn't make a dent. The news that his birth father was one of the wealthiest cattle ranchers in Texas had hit like a rogue wave in a calm sea, obliterating everything in its path. As it turned out, being a McGannon was news.

Kurt McGannon? He tried the name on for size. Nope. Couldn't do it. Not even for a million bucks. Kurt's last name had been Johnson for the past thirty-five years and he wasn't about to change it now. The other one didn't sound right, plus there was the fact that he didn't want to be a McGannon.

Taking the call from a stranger claiming to be Kurt's uncle was the first mistake. Since the article came out, his work cell hadn't stopped ringing. Reporters. People claiming to be relatives. After being an orphan for the past couple of years, Kurt had been informed that he had six siblings and five cousins. Don't even get him started on the uncle who'd pulled him into this mess in the first place. The man had summoned Kurt to the hospital to drop the bomb on Kurt's newfound siblings that their father had cheated on their mother.

So, that pretty much made him the most popular guy in the place and begged the question…what had he gotten himself into?

The condition of Kurt's birth father seemed dire. Clive McGannon was in a coma after an accident left him with a head injury. Kurt figured that it was just his luck to find out that he had a father under these weird circumstances.

The whole part about the man being one of the richest in Texas was going to take a while to process. Kurt didn't want or need another person's money. He'd earned plenty of his own. Granted, he wasn't McGannon family rich, but his storage business provided enough to bring up his daughter with food on the table and a solid roof over her head. He had enough for extras, like vacations and extracurriculars.

His problem wasn't financial. Ever since that article appeared in the Houston Daily News, both print and online versions no less, Kurt's life was blowing up. Work phone. Inbox. It didn't stop there. Calls from banks, lawyers, and a persistent millionaire matchmaker service poured in. All claiming to have his best interest at heart. Right. If he believed that someone probably had a bridge to sell him, too.

Kurt had never been more grateful for his personal cell phone. Only a handful of people had been given the number. He kept his private cell with him at all times in case his babysitter needed to reach him.

He glanced toward the kitchen as he made another lap around the living room. More frustration seethed and that meant he needed to go hard on a workout. He passed the kitchen table on his way to the garage where he'd set up a home gym in the second parking space.

Popping an earbud in his left ear, he scrolled through his tunes before settling on AC/DC's Thunderstruck.

His workout started slow, and he couldn't seem to get it going. No number of push-ups could make him stop thinking about his surprise family or the chaos that headline was causing in his life. To be honest, it wasn't just the news distracting him. Levi McGannon, the oldest of the siblings, had reached out yesterday to set up a family meeting so they could get to know each other better. Kurt had yet to return that call.

Since push-ups to classic rock weren't doing the trick, he jumped to standing and grabbed a jump rope. It didn't take four rotations for the rope to catch on his feet. He untangled it and started again. This time, he didn't make it two jumps without the darn thing snagging on his ankles.

Time to put away the rope. His concentration was shot as he ran through the rest his workout routine. Twenty minutes in and a lot of starts and stops, he decided to hang it up. His dog, Cuzya, would be up by now, ready for her turn to exercise. She usually slept upstairs in his daughter's room. His babysitter, Ms. Calaway, stayed in the adjoining room during the week.

Paisley was a good sleeper and it was way too early for her to wake up, but Kurt would never get a decent sweat going if she surprised him before he got out the door. He grabbed Cuzya's leash and headed up the stairwell to his daughter's bedroom to get his dog.

He jingled the leash as he neared the top. Cuzya came trotting out.

"Good, girl," he whispered, taking a knee and scratching her behind the ears. No way would he risk waking his angel when he was this close to getting in a much-needed run.

Leashing his dog, he slipped out of the house and onto the front porch. He locked the door behind them before shooting off a quick text to let Ms. Calaway know what he was up to. Sitting on the porch, he laced up his running shoes.

It was five o'clock in the morning, still dark. He always got up early to work out before starting the day. Now, he had questions about where his habits came from.

Did he wake up early every day because he had rancher's blood? Was he successful because of his father's shared DNA? Had his father somehow helped him along?

It was crazy how uncertain he'd become after a quick trip to a hospital in Katy Gulch Texas, an even quicker swab, and a DNA test.

Kurt tried to convince himself he didn't care who his father was. The man was nothing more than a sperm donor. He hadn't been around for Kurt or his mother during his childhood. There'd been no child support payments. Kurt's mother had struggled to make ends meet at times. High school graduation? Party of two, three if he counted Stacy. He and his high school sweetheart married the summer after graduation and life together had been good. They'd decided to hold off on having a family while they got their acts together and could handle the responsibility. He'd launched a successful business while she'd worked her way through community college and became a graphic designer. She'd designed the company website and had learned how to handle much of the finances while he'd tracked down business. The two of them had made a great team.

Kurt's mom had passed away before Stacy got pregnant and then he lost his wife, too. Paisley was the only family he had.

And that brought him to the present. Kurt wouldn't have even gone to the trouble to respond to the call from a random guy who called himself Kurt's uncle a year ago when Stacy was alive. But she'd had no contact with her parents after their divorce. He was an orphan. If anything happened to him, their daughter, Paisley, would be an orphan.

His moment of weakness in returning the call from a stranger had resulted in finding out he was part of a large family—one he wasn't all that sure he wanted, and one that couldn't possibly want him around.

Granted, they'd extended a welcome once the results came in at the hospital and, much to Kurt's shock, they seemed genuine. Under different circumstances, they seemed like the kind of people Kurt would actually like.

But their offer of family had to be a Trojan horse. And, thanks to his high school Lit teacher, he knew exactly how that had turned out.

So, yeah, he wasn't going down that road only to be wiped out no matter how authentic they seemed on the surface.

As much as he wanted Paisley to have a family that extended beyond him, he couldn't risk her getting attached only to be hurt. She'd lost enough for one lifetime. And she'd only been on the earth a little more than a year.

That little girl was his world and vice versa. He figured she had a right to know if she had a bigger family out there. She would want to know. Wouldn't she?

So much of parenting was blind guesswork. It was a lot like being told to change the oil in his motorcycle while blindfolded and without any tools.

Kurt smacked his palms against his cement porch before pushing up to standing. Cuzya's tail was working double time in anticipation of the run. That's all he wanted to focus on. Not the fact that he might've gotten an early riser gene from his father because his mother couldn't get out of bed before nine to save her life.

So, there he was…wondering if he'd gotten traits from a father he'd never met.

By this hour, he usually dripped from sweat after a vigorous forty-five-minute workout. Out of courtesy, if he saw anyone coming toward him at the park, he'd be sure to pivot around them so they wouldn't get caught in his airstream. No one deserved that. Not even the woman who brought her immaculately groomed white standard poodle to the park and gave anyone stink-eye who tried to let their dog get anywhere near her white furball. Kurt would swear both the woman and her dog kept their noses pointed toward the sky so they wouldn't have to make eye contact with 'normal' people. Maybe they deserved to smell him, but no other innocent bystander should endure that curse.

The real question coming next was whether he planned to move forward with his family. This was exactly the kind of thing he would've asked Stacy about and she would've had the right answer. His wife always knew the right path, whereas Kurt felt like he was alone in a canoe paddling left.

Losing his wife had felt like cement poured around his heart. He'd been devastated and unsure how to move on or breathe right up until the nurse asked him if he wanted to meet his daughter.

Having his daughter placed in his arms had been a game-changer. He went from a deep sense of loss to an even deeper sense of purpose.

It was impossible not to worry he would be letting Paisley and Stacy down by closing her off to the possibility of being part of a large family. In the few short hours he'd been around the McGannons, it was easy to see they were a tightknit bunch. But would they accept an outsider like his daughter?

Kurt couldn't care less if they approved of him. Hurt his child and there was no end to which he wouldn't go to bring pain to their doorstep. So, he was caught between a rock and a hard place on this one. And he wished like hell he could just tap into a magic line and ask his wife.

There were two labels that Kurt hated, widower and orphan. He bore both.

He grabbed Cuzya's leash, the Rhodesian ridgeback's ears perked up. She might be eight years old, but she acted like two.

"Come on, girl," he urged.

Her tail wagged double time. Morning runs were her favorite and he could swear she was smiling as she looked up at him.

Kurt took off toward the park, a familiar route for Cuzya. The seventy-five-pound animal trotted easily beside him. This pace was nothing for her, but it was good to warm up her muscles before hitting their stride.

AC/DC roared through Kurt's earbud into his left ear. He'd always been a vintage rock anthem guy. Back in Black was his all-time favorite song. He liked the guitar riffs, and the beat made him want to get up and move. Then there was Angus Young, shredding on the guitar.

Not even his go-to song could shake his sour mood.

Three laps around the park had Cuzya warmed up and ready to go. Kurt couldn't find his stride no matter how hard he tried. Running might have his heart rate up but wasn't exactly helping with his mindset. At least he was sweating now.

His phone went off, causing his pulse to skyrocket. No one ever contacted him this time of the morning. His first thought was that a reporter had somehow gotten hold of the number. His second, an attorney. Several seemed very interested in 'helping' him claim his part of the McGannon fortune.

Kurt stopped running as he pulled his cell out of the pouch strapped to his arm. He hit the mute button on his music and checked the screen.

His chest squeezed and it was hard to breathe when he read the name, Ms. Calaway. Why would his sitter call at this time if not for an emergency?

"Is something wrong with Paisley?" He didn't bother with a greeting as he heard his daughter wailing in the background.

This was bad. So bad. An invisible knot tightened in his chest, making it hard to breathe.

"There was a man..." His sitter spoke in between gasps. He could scarcely hear her over his daughter's cries. "He tried..."

"To what? Take her?" was all he could ask as he turned tail and backtracked toward home. His worst fear played out in his mind as he waited for a response from his sitter and his heart battered his rib cage.

"No. I-didn't-he-couldn't—"

"She's safe?"

"Yes," she managed to say through gulps of air.

"You're okay?"

"Ambulance." The one word sent a ripple of fear through his body. Kurt hated hospitals more than almost anything.

"Are you home?" he asked.

"I—"

The voice of his neighbor, Mr. Rodriguez, came on the line. "I forgot to take my garbage to the curb last night, so I hurried to get it out before the truck came this morning. That's when I heard a scream. I looked over at your house and saw a shadow move across your front window. I got a bad feeling when I didn't hear Cuzya bark, so I ran inside my house to get my shotgun from the closet."

His quick thinking might have just saved Paisley's life.

"By the time I got to your house," he continued, "a man had knocked Bea over and had Paisley in his arms."

"And now?" Kurt realized Paisley was okay. Her cries could be heard loud and clear and they made him turn up the gas as he ran, ignoring burning thighs, to get to his baby girl.

"I got here just in time," Mr. Rodriguez said on a sigh. "Bea took a hard hit and I already called for the cops and an ambulance. But he got away."

"Can you stay with them?" Kurt asked, scanning the street for any other runners.

"Yes. Of course," Mr. Rodriguez said.

"I'll be there as fast as I can," Kurt said through short bursts of air. He ended the call as he poured on the gas.

Rounding the corner two blocks from his house, sirens pierced the air. A few seconds later, a squad car ripped past him. An ambulance soon followed. By the time he reached home, a swarm had descended on his three-bedroom craftsman.

The back of an ambulance and two squad cars were aimed at his front door. Since the situation was volatile, and he didn't want to end up shot, he put his hands high in the air where they could easily be seen as he beat feet toward his front yard.

"This is my house," he shouted to a cop on the front porch.

The officer turned around, keeping his hand on the butt of the gun in its holster. "Sir, you need to stop right there."

"I live here. That's my daughter in there." Kurt's plea was met with a sympathetic look, but the officer didn't give any indication that he was going to budge. "I can prove it."

It was then that he realized he didn't have his driver's license on him or his wallet. All he had was his cell phone.

2

"**S**tay right there, sir. I'll call my supervising officer." The cop identified himself as Officer Tanner Forth before turning his face toward his left shoulder and speaking over the radio.

"I'm not going anywhere." Kurt stood on the sidewalk. More of that sweat poured from his face and body, soaking his shirt. His pulse was through the roof as he could hear Paisley from the street. He shifted his weight and flexed and released his fingers a few times, trying to work out the stress. The only things keeping him from violating the cop's order was the gun on his side and the fact that Paisley was safe.

Kurt couldn't fathom what might've happened if his neighbor hadn't decided to take out his trash at the exact moment he did. Standing there, heaving for air, the knot in Kurt's chest tightened again.

A few seconds later, the front door opened, and Mr. Rodriguez leaned out. Paisley was on his hip but kept her shielded behind the door. He looked at the officer and immediately nodded. "That's her father."

"Sir, you may approach. I apologize—"

"No need." Kurt bolted toward his neighbor. At some point he would figure out how to repay the man for saving his daughter's and Ms. Calaway's lives but right now all he could think about was holding his baby girl.

Mr. Rodriguez met Kurt halfway on the porch. The minute Paisley's gaze zeroed in on him, her tears doubled, and she leaned toward him with outstretched arms. The incident had understandably traumatized her.

In that moment, like so many others, she reminded him so much of her mother with those big blue eyes and blonde curls. He held her tightly against his chest. Her little hands pressed against his neck as she held onto him for dear life.

Paisley had the same wheat-colored hair as Stacy and eyes that were usually like looking at glass. Now, red-rimmed, they nearly broke Kurt's heart as he searched for words to comfort his daughter.

"It's okay. Daddy's here. You're safe." Kurt said other words meant to soothe his daughter as she cried so hard that she hiccupped. Words felt hollow. He hadn't been there when she needed him most. The sense of letting her down, of letting Stacy down, was almost crippling.

Obviously, calming his daughter was his priority right now. Make no mistake about it, he had every intention of tracking down the bastard who'd violated his home, hurt his babysitter and tried to take his daughter away.

"How's Ms. Calaway?" he asked his neighbor before offering a handshake.

"She took a hit to the head and a pretty hard fall. The good news is she was sitting up and talking when I walked out here," he said.

The front door opened, and they all had to step aside so a gurney carrying his babysitter could be rolled across the porch. Blood stained the white sheet that had been placed over Ms. Calaway. A gash marked her forehead where she took the hit. The minute she saw Kurt, she tried to speak through the oxygen mask covering her mouth.

"It's okay. She's safe. You're going to be taken good care of at the hospital. I've got everything covered at home. You just focus on healing. Okay?" Relief washed over him as he saw her, sitting up and trying to talk. He had every intention of making certain that her hospital bill came to him directly.

She seemed to contemplate his words for a second, and he almost expected her to put up an argument. But she didn't. Instead, she gave a resigned nod.

Kurt looked to an EMT with the nametag, John. "She's going to be okay, right?"

"We're going to take good care of her for you, sir." John nodded and winked as he navigated the gurney down the steps on the porch along with his co-worker. The reassurance kept Kurt from jumping into his truck and trying to follow them to the hospital.

That, and the fact Ms. Calaway was lucid, settled his nerves. Shaken, but she was fundamentally awake and alert. All good signs she would recover from this ordeal. Emotional scars were a different story altogether. He'd take it one step at a time with her.

"She had me call her niece to cover for her," Mr. Rodriguez explained as Officer Forth took notes.

Kurt watched as his babysitter was loaded into the back of an ambulance. The knot in his chest tightened at thinking he'd done something to expose her to the attack.

"That's not necessary," Kurt responded to his neighbor. Paisley's sobs had morphed into soft cries and the occasional hiccup as he rubbed her back. "I won't be needing a sitter today."

"Sir, I have a few questions for you if you have a few minutes," Officer Forth said.

Kurt glanced around. There were a couple of neighbors out on the front porch, no doubt wondering what all the commotion was about. They watched as the ambulance doors closed with Ms. Calaway secured inside.

The vehicle kept its siren off—another good sign because it meant the driver wasn't in a panic to get her to the hospital—and then drove away.

"Yes, of course. We can go inside if you'd like." Kurt motioned toward the door after scanning the area for any signs the bastards had decided to stick around and watch what happened next or look for an opportunity to try again.

Kurt turned to Mr. Rodriguez. "You can call and cancel her niece because—"

"Arianna," Mr. Rodriguez supplied.

"Okay, you can call off Arianna. I have no intention of leaving my daughter today." He didn't feel the need to add, *with a stranger, because that part had to be obvious.*

His neighbor was quick and seemed to catch on. He gave an understanding nod. As much as Kurt trusted Ms. Calaway with his life, and he figured her niece was more than capable for stepping in for her, he just needed to be with his child right now.

"I have no way of contacting her. Bea handed me her phone and told me what contact to find after I called 9-1-1. You can tell her to go away, but I have no way of reaching her before she gets here." Mr. Rodriguez threw his hands up as he apologized.

"Don't worry about it. I appreciate everything you've done for my family. Thank you from the bottom of my heart. I can't think about what would've happened if you hadn't stepped in when you did. Would you like to come inside for a cup of coffee?" Kurt asked.

Officer Forth opened the screen door. "I'd like to hear more details of what happened, Mr. Rodriguez. If I can get a few moments of your time."

"Yes, sir," he said to the officer before turning to Kurt. "A cup of coffee sounds good to me."

As he lifted his hand to take the door from Officer Forth, the older man's hand shook. Anger roared through Kurt when he thought about the fact someone had broken into his home to take his daughter. Words couldn't express his frustration that he'd been away from home when it had gone down. A thought struck. Had that been the plan all along? Had someone been watching the house? A chill raced down his spine.

Inside, another officer took pictures as he moved around the living room. An end table had been turned over along with its contents. The officer introduced himself with a handshake before declaring, "I got what I needed. I'm on my way out."

Kurt thanked the officer as him and Officer Forth huddled up, no doubt sharing information.

"The kitchen is this way," Kurt said to Raul. It didn't take long for Officer Forth to join them.

"Do you want to sit in your highchair for a minute?" Kurt asked Paisley. Her response came immediately in the form of a death grip on his arm. He could only imagine how confusing and scary this ordeal must've been for her.

The thought he'd let his daughter, and Stacy, down in the worst possible way caused that knot to tighten again. It had been there ever since his wife died and it was like some invisible person stood to either side of Kurt, playing a game of tug of war when anything happened that could possibly hurt their daughter.

So, when a knock sounded and then the front door opened, he was ruder than he probably should have been.

"Who are you and what are you doing here?" He moved to the doorway so he could see better.

"My name is Arianna Ballard." The stunning woman who stepped into his living room caused his heart to skip a beat.

"Sorry." He searched for the name and came up empty. "Who?"

"BEA CALAWAY IS MY AUNT," Arianna clarified. The guy holding the baby must be Kurt Johnson, her aunt's employer.

"Sorry, come on in," a second man waved her in from behind Kurt.

Considering everything that had happened, she wasn't exactly put off by her aunt's employer's reaction to her. He held onto his child fiercely and possessively, like if anyone tried to get anywhere near her...lights out.

"I've been trying to call my aunt's phone and I haven't gotten a response. She had a neighbor call and leave a message, asking me to come over and sit for her. Does anyone have an update on her?"

"My name is Raul Rodriguez. I'm the one who called on your aunt's behalf." The older gentleman met her halfway as Kurt held tighter to his daughter before turning his attention back to an officer, who made his presence known in the kitchen.

"I don't have an update on your aunt, except that I know she took a blow to the head and—"

"Wait. Hold on a minute." Arianna couldn't have possibly heard him right. "Did you say a blow to the head? I thought she fell or something."

The squad car outside should've clued her in this was more than a fall. It had sent a warning flare and riled her up, but she couldn't fathom anything actually happening.

"Before you get too worried, your aunt was awake and alert when she left here in the ambulance," Raul said.

"Ambulance?" she parroted.

"That's right. She had enough presence of mind to hand me her phone and tell me to call you. The EMT promised to take good care of her and her prognosis seemed good. She was understandably shaken up," Raul explained. "She's a very strong woman."

"Thank you for letting me know." She twisted her hands together. Raul was just about one of the kindest men Ariana had ever met. "She's important. She's basically all the family I have left. I figured if she was sending me here, she didn't need me at the hospital. It sounds

19

like you know my aunt so I don't have to tell you that she can be pretty stubborn when she wants to be. She would, of course, take care of a child in her care and forget about herself."

Raul was rocking his head in agreement. "That's the Bea Calaway I know."

She nodded toward the kitchen. "What about him? My aunt only says nice things about him but that's her way. Is he as decent as she claims?"

"I know him about as well as you do, I'm afraid. Bea wouldn't work for a jerk and he's always been a friendly enough neighbor despite keeping to himself mostly."

Arianna wasn't so sure that Kurt Johnson was as nice as her aunt had made him out to be. But then, based on the emergency phone call she'd received from Raul, she'd expected to walk into a stressful situation. Not this.

"How was my aunt injured?" She breathed slowly, trying to bring oxygen to starved lungs.

"A man broke in and tried to kidnap Paisley. Bea put herself in the way and was knocked over."

Arianna gasped. She brought her hand to cover her mouth as her pulse skyrocketed. "Oh, no. My aunt. And poor Paisley. I had no idea. I'm so sorry. You said that my aunt is going to be okay?"

"She looked like it on the way out of here. Every precaution is being taken with her." His words offered a measure of reassurance. The overwhelming urge to reach for her cell phone to call her aunt came over her. Hearing her aunt's voice would go a long way toward easing Arianna's anxiety.

Kurt must be a nervous wreck thinking about what might have happened to his daughter. His actions made a lot more sense to her now.

"We're about to give statements to the officer back there in the kitchen. Would you like to join us?" Raul asked.

"Yes, thank you." She followed him, ignoring how much her temperature raised being in the same room with Kurt.

The craftsman home was clean, orderly and minimally decorated, just as she remembered from the few times she'd been there. The place had a warm and friendly vibe with just enough brightly colored toys and blankets to know a family lived here. Her aunt had said there was no mother in the picture. She'd hinted at tragedy but never gave away her employer's secrets.

There were a couple pictures of Paisley as a baby. None of Kurt. Not surprising since he was most likely the one behind the camera. There were no pictures of a woman with the baby, leading Arianna to think there was no mother in the picture at all.

There was one photo of a very pregnant woman holding her belly and smiling at the camera. The look of love in her eyes was a shot straight to Arianna's heart. Was the lack of photographs after the birth due to something tragic happening, like her aunt had hinted at? Again, Aunt Bea never said one way or the other. And yet, a picture was emerging—one that broke Arianna's heart.

"So, you know as much as I do at this point, Officer Forth," Kurt said. He glanced over at her as she came into the room and something unfamiliar passed behind his eyes. Her pulse spiked and she had to remind herself to breathe.

Kurt was taller than her aunt had described, and he had muscles stacked on top of muscles. He also had the whole chiseled jaw bit down along with the most serious set of dark roast eyes. Her traitorous heart gave a little flip when he looked at her and heat flooded her body. Despite the circumstances, she felt a strong physical attraction to him.

The officer had a small notebook and a pencil in hand, taking notes. Arianna figured Kurt probably needed help with the baby, so she walked over to her favorite little curly-headed toddler and put her hands out.

Paisley smiled through red-rimmed eyes. She sat up straight before tilting her body toward Arianna, shocking her father in the move.

"Hold on there." Kurt took a step away, making it impossible for Arianna to reach Paisley.

What did Arianna do wrong and why did the move of him jerking backward feel like a slap in the face?

3

"**U**h, sorry, I was trying to help. I thought this is what my aunt wanted. I thought it might be easier for you to talk to the officer if I took her. But, it's okay. You can hold her while I...clean up the kitchen or something useful." Confused, she dropped her arms.

Brow furrowed, Kurt said, "I'm the one who's sorry. It's just that she doesn't normally take to strangers."

"I'm not. We've met." And then it dawned on her that he probably had no idea that she already had a relationship with his daughter. "I meet my aunt and your daughter at the park for picnic lunches sometimes."

She was at least a little surprised that her aunt hadn't mentioned her to him at all. She smiled at Paisley, so the little girl wouldn't be too thrown by her father's action. The two couldn't look more opposite. Paisley with her kinky curls and light eyes, whereas his hair was so dark it was almost black. The baby was all softness and giggles whereas he was intense with a face of hard angles and sharp planes. The little girl had cuteness down pat. Her father was intense and...sexy. Yeah, the man was hotness on a stick. What could Arianna say? He was bone-melting handsome. And she was certain he had his pick in the dating pool.

"Ms. Calaway meets her niece for lunch at the park. As in little girl." He held out his left hand, palm to the floor, about four feet high.

She tilted her head to the side. "I'm a little bit taller than that. And it's me that she's been meeting, not a little kid."

Well, that news seemed to set the man back. She could almost see the wheels turning in the back of his mind. It shouldn't amuse her that she'd thrown him for a loop, but it did.

Then, she got a handle on her emotions because this wasn't the time or place given the circumstances.

He shook his head like he was shaking off the possibility of being wrong. "I guess I thought because it was a park and lunch that she was talking about a kid. I didn't realize she was talking about a grown woman."

It wasn't what he said so much as how he said it that got under her skin.

"Well, for your information, my aunt and I are close. Like I said to Raul, it's just the two of us in our family. So, if you think it's juvenile that I meet my aunt in a playground I can't help you, especially as the reason we go there in the first place is because your daughter likes the swings."

"She likes the swings?" he asked.

"Yes." She started cooling off when his tone changed. "She loves it when we push her and sing this ridiculous song to her that my aunt made up. But if you find me offensive—"

"I didn't say that," he countered quickly. And that was the second sign she didn't think he was a complete jerk. The first was how tightly he held onto his daughter, like someone would have to move heaven and earth to pry that little girl out of his arms.

Arianna shouldn't let herself get so defensive around him. She'd never felt so on edge around a stranger before and she reminded herself to get a grip.

Plus, her aunt had always talked so nicely about Kurt. She spoke about him like he was an angel. The fact he was angry and short with her probably had thrown her off-kilter. She was catching him after what had to be any parent's worst nightmare. If Aunt Bea liked him,

Kurt Johnson had to be a good person. Her aunt had always been a great judge of character.

He also had a pretty great little girl. He couldn't be a complete jerk or there was no way Paisley would be turning out as great as she was. So, Arianna decided to cut him slack on their chilly introduction.

"I'm sorry," he finally said after standing there, stunned, like he didn't know what to say to her after the snub.

"Don't worry about it. I can put on coffee if anyone wants it." She knew where supplies were, having stopped in for coffee a few times.

"Coffee would be great." At least he'd softened his tone. "Three cups if it's no trouble."

"None at all." She casually lifted a shoulder like it was no big deal, and it wasn't. She wanted to make herself useful.

Arianna went to work, fixing each coffee cup. He had one of those pod machines, which meant making them one by one. She didn't mind. She listened as Raul brought the officer up to speed. She flinched at hearing the fact someone had tried to abduct Paisley. Worse yet, from her home.

Kurt's actions were making a whole lot more sense to her as she listened to the story as it unfolded. The horror of someone breaking in and trying to take a child from her own home hit Arianna deeply.

He'd relaxed the tense muscles of his face after he'd realized she was supposed to be there. Now that she realized what had happened, she understood his concern at her walking in the front door like she owned the place.

Standing there brooding, the man was intense.

"Is there anyone you can think of, Mr. Johnson, who might have a grudge against you?" Officer Forth asked.

Kurt issued a sharp breath. "A week ago, I found out that my birth father was Clive McGannon. I have six brothers and five cousins, none of whom saw this news coming and an uncle who seemed more than happy to stir the pot and get everyone riled up."

Kurt Johnson's father was the Clive McGannon? Well, that put a whole new spin on the situation.

"Did any of them threaten you or your daughter?" the officer asked.

"No, sir. In fact, when the DNA test revealed paternity, they each took turns welcoming me into the family."

KURT REMEMBERED *the scene like it was yesterday instead of a little more than a week ago. He explained to the officer that he'd shown up at the hospital after receiving a call from someone claiming to be his uncle. Donny McGannon summoned Kurt to County General but warned him that he might not receive a warm reception.*

At first, Kurt wrote off the old man as crazy and tried to put the information out of his mind. It was too late. The information got inside his head. At first, he thought about the fact he was Paisley's only living relative. He thought about her being shifted into foster care should anything happen to him.

The thought of a safety net, for her sake, was too much to pass up. He'd decided to make the hour and a half trip to feel the situation out and see if his so-called family members were decent people.

Walking into the hospital had brought back a flood of memories—none of them good. Seeing his beloved Stacy in the hospital bed...lifeless...gone...

Kurt cleared the emotion clotting in his throat at the memory. Images crashed down on him harder than a loose boulder on a winding mountain road. There'd been no warning signs for the emotions that had threatened to cripple him the day he learned Stacy wasn't coming home. She would never hold the daughter she wanted so badly. She would never read the bedtime stories from the books she'd bought to fill the nursery. She would never rock the baby in the chair she'd meticulously picked out.

Even a year later, thinking about her and all the milestones she was missing—and would miss as Paisley grew up—threatened to drag him under. He'd been so close to being pulled out with the riptide in those early days. Kurt missed his wife. There were no words to describe the pain he'd stuffed down so deep he feared it made him a volcano ready to erupt with the right trigger.

Looking back, his introduction to the McGannons had gotten off to a bad start because of it. Setting foot inside the hospital had messed with his head. He'd been avoiding medical centers like the plague since his wife's death.

Meeting his half-siblings in that emotional state hadn't exactly been his best play. Again, he'd had no idea what to expect and hadn't expected to be thrust into their lives in a hospital while waiting to hear news as to whether or not their father was about to wake up from the coma he'd been in for weeks.

To say the meeting was tense was a lot like saying habanero peppers were a little hot.

"Do you think any of the members of the McGannon family could be responsible for the attempted kidnapping?" Officer Forth asked.

"No." Blaming one of them would be an easy answer but they didn't strike him as the type to do something so dirty.

Kurt glanced at Ms. Calaway's niece, who'd busied herself setting up breakfast of diced fruit, dry cereal and a sippy cup of milk for Paisley. Cuzya seemed content to settle in next to Paisley. He walked over to the highchair. Arianna's smile sent a warning shot to his heart as she pulled the tray off so he could set Paisley in the chair.

The woman was beautiful. More so than he wanted to acknowledge at the moment. She was tall and her legs went on for days. Her black-as-night hair hung halfway down her back looking like a thick braided rope. Her creamy skin caused his fingers to flex, wanting to reach out to touch the wispy hairs that framed her face. And just forget about those cherry lips on an oval-shaped face.

Arianna Ballard caused his pulse to skyrocket. She was the perfect mix of smart, sensual, and determined. Kurt counted himself a good judge of character and he was impressed by Ms. Calaway's niece.

As soon as Paisley was settled, Arianna asked the little girl, "Who's hungry?"

"Me." That one word. That big smile. Kurt's heart took a second hit at his daughter's reaction to Arianna. He chalked it up to the fact Paisley hadn't had a mother figure in her life. Ms. Calaway was the grandmother Paisley needed. He wasn't as shocked to see the two of them bond easily.

But then Ms. Calaway had been with him and Paisley since the day he brought her home.

"I'll need a list of friends and acquaintances. Write down anyone you've been in a disagreement with," Officer Forth said.

Kurt moved to the junk drawer in his kitchen and retrieved a pad of paper and pen.

"Care to sit?" He motioned toward the four-top table.

"Yes, thank you." The officer looked at Kurt's neighbor. "Thank you for your statement, sir. Call the station if you remember anything else that seems important."

"Will do, Officer." Before Raul excused himself, he said, "I'm heading up to the hospital to check on Bea. I'll give you an update as soon as I hear anything new."

"Here's my number." Kurt rattled it off as Raul added the contact.

Holding up his phone, he said, "I got it."

"I appreciate it." Kurt couldn't let himself go there with the scenario that Raul didn't pick the exact moment he did to take the trash out. A lucky coincidence but one he'd take.

"Would you like to come with me?" he asked Arianna.

"My aunt wanted me to stay here for Paisley." She chewed on her bottom lip and shifted her weight, like she hated picking one over the other.

"I can bring you up later," Kurt offered.

"Thank you," she said to him.

Raul let himself out as Kurt finished the list of people. He couldn't think of the people who worked for him, his people, as suspects.

"What about socially? Is there anyone who might be upset with you?" The officer asked.

"As in a girlfriend?" Kurt balked. Between his one year old and owning a business, he didn't have a lot of time for socializing. He was lucky to catch a game on TV over the weekend. And for some odd reason, he looked to Arianna when he answered.

Kurt didn't want to get inside his head about what that glance meant. He picked up his cup of coffee and rolled the mug around in his hands, trying to shake off the question.

"No, sir. I'm a widower." Kurt hated labels. He'd picked up quite a few. Orphan. Single father. Widower. Those were top of mind.

"What kind of work do you do?" Officer Forth nodded as he made a note.

"I own a business." Kurt described his temporary storage solutions company.

"Have you fired anyone lately or would anyone have a grievance against you?" Forth asked.

"No, and not that I know of," he said.

"Would you mind providing a list of employees?" Forth continued.

"Not at all." Kurt had to grab his cell phone to retrieve the full list, none of whom he believed would have a reason to have a problem with him. Trying to abduct his daughter was a serious message. Guilt racked him that he hadn't been in the office much in the past year. He was out of touch with his people and he needed to get back in the saddle when it came to his business considering he didn't recognize a few of the names in the file.

Was he that out of touch? Logic said he was no matter how much he didn't want to believe he could've let his responsibilities slip to that degree.

"My top guy is Devin Sparks. I've been working from home most of the past year. He can fill you in on the work environment better than I can. And then there's Rory Smith, who is his second in command," he said.

"And neither of these people hold a grudge against you?"

"Not that I know of." He hadn't spoken to Rory in far too long. Devin stopped by weekly to provide updates. He seemed stressed lately and that was because his wife was due with their first child soon. Anxiousness and late-term first pregnancies seemed to go hand-in-hand.

"You haven't had any disagreements with clients or anyone outside of work lately, right? Neighbors?" Officer Forth asked.

Based on the way Arianna had looked at him when she first stepped into the kitchen, he could surmise that she wasn't particularly fond of him. Since they'd just met and he probably deserved the death glares, he decided to keep that name to himself.

The officer finished up, asking a few more routine-sounding questions. He pulled a business card from his pocket and set it down on the table.

"If anyone comes up that you forgot to mention, I'd appreciate a call." Officer Forth stood up. He was thicker than he was tall, coming in almost a solid foot shorter than Kurt. At six-foot-five-inches, most people didn't measure up to Kurt's height. Not even in Texas where it felt like six-foot was the average male height.

"Yes, sir." Kurt stood, too. He followed the officer to the front door.

"I'll canvas your neighbors to get a sense if anyone saw anything," he said.

Kurt never saw any lights on, but it was worth a shot.

"Thank you for following up on this," Kurt said. He shook the officer's hand before closing the door behind him.

By the time he returned to the kitchen, Arianna was singing Paisley's favorite song to her. His heart squeezed and the knot twisted. Seeing his daughter laughing with a female wasn't something he'd witnessed outside of Ms. Calaway and that was different. His babysitter was old enough to be Paisley's grandmother.

Arianna was closer to a mother's age.

Kurt shook off the emotion pressing heavy on his chest. He cleared his throat to announce that he was coming into the room, unsure why he suddenly felt like he was trespassing in his own home.

"Thanks for coming," he started.

She whirled around on him like she was gearing up for a fight. It dawned on him that she must think that he was about to kick her out.

"I hope you'll stay," he said before she could form a protest. And his heart felt a little too right when he said those words.

4

"**M**y aunt sent me to cover for her. I'm here as long as you need me." Arianna folded her arms and studied Kurt. The man looked like he could use some kindness about then. "I know we were introduced earlier, but I didn't get a chance to say that it's nice to meet you. My aunt has said a lot of nice things about you."

The corners of his mouth turned up in a small smile and he was devastatingly handsome. Having recently gotten out of a relationship with a divorced man—or so she'd believed he was divorced until she found out the truth—the last thing she wanted or needed was to be attracted to another single father.

Corbitt had been convincing. She had to give that much to her ex. Finding out that he'd been cheating on his wife with Arianna had knocked the wind out of her. Aside from the embarrassment and humiliation, she'd been surprisingly okay with their relationship ending once she got over the anger. She never would have dated a married man if she'd known. It broke every rule she'd ever had for herself. As it turned out, the real pain of the breakup came from how attached she'd become to his two-year-old daughter, Kiara.

So, yeah, dating a guy with a kid wasn't high on her list. A breakup was hard enough with two people involved. Add a kid in the mix and it could be devastating. She wasn't falling down that rabbit hole again with anyone.

"Your aunt is right up there as one of my all-time favorite people," he admitted. "Paisley loves her, too."

Hearing those words wasn't helping her dislike the man as much as she wanted to.

"The feeling is mutual," Arianna said before adding, "with my aunt."

Kurt rubbed the scruff on his chin. The day-old stubble only added to his good looks. So, the not being attracted to him thing wasn't exactly off to a good start.

But it didn't matter. A date wasn't exactly on the table and her main focus was on keeping Paisley safe. Speaking of which…

"I heard Raul tell the officer what happened. What are the chances the guy will come back?" she asked.

"With all the confusion and just trying to keep my daughter safe, it didn't occur to me that he would," he admitted. He took a lap around the kitchen before stopping to stare out the window over the sink. "But I'd be naïve to think that it wasn't at least a possibility. I need to plan for the worst-case scenario in order to protect everyone here."

For a split-second, standing there, he looked like a lost little boy. And that was the only thing boyish about him. Kurt Johnson was all man. He didn't strike her as the kind of person who would take the breach of his own home lightly. She could tell after spending an hour with him what kind of person he was. Strong-willed. Determined. Protective. Intense. Those were a few words that came to mind when she thought about describing him to others.

"I saw the front door. I'm guessing that's how they got in," she said.

He raked his hand through his thick hair. Slowly, he nodded. "I need to go board that up to stop anyone else from getting the same idea. Actually, I have a better idea."

He walked over to his cell phone that he'd placed on the kitchen table. He picked it up and made a quick call.

"Henry, think you can swing by? I have an emergency window break in my front door that needs fixing. I could also use a second

deadbolt lock. Maybe something installed low that can't easily be reached with a broken window." He paused a beat. "A key lock sounds like it would do the trick."

There was silence as Kurt rocked his head.

"That would be...I'd appreciate it...I definitely owe you one." Another beat passed. "You ever need a favor; all you have to do is name it." Kurt thanked the guy on the other end of the line before ending the call.

"Henry is planning to swing by in the next hour." He turned toward Arianna and locked gazes. They held on a few seconds and she took another hit square in the chest. An attraction between the two of them was out of the question. Actually, the attraction was biology. Reason and logic came into the picture when deciding whether or not to act on it.

There'd be no acting on her part. She didn't even need to remind herself that this gorgeous man had a child, which made him off limits after her recent breakup. But it was more than that. There was something dangerous about him that she hadn't experienced with anyone else. Not once in her life did someone from the opposite sex have this big of an impact on her within minutes of meeting. Her internal warning systems told her this guy could break her heart.

"That's good. That'll be a huge help in securing the place," she said, tamping down those thoughts.

"I'm not done yet." Again, their gazes locked. "I won't stop until I'm a thousand percent sure it's safe. Not just for my daughter but for your aunt. I intend to provide an environment where she feels safe."

"I appreciate the reassurance. There's no way my aunt would quit or leave you stranded in case you're worried," she said.

He seemed offended and that made her feel like a jerk.

"I appreciate everything that your aunt does for us. I don't really look at her like someone who works for me. She's family. She spends every day with the most important person in my life and manages to make my daughter feel like there's another person in the world who cares enough to step into harm's way for her. I'm not really worried about your aunt quitting. If she didn't feel safe here, I'd want her to leave because she matters to us and I want her to feel comfortable," he defended.

Arianna had put her foot in her mouth. She'd misjudged him from the minute they met, and she wasn't trying to put more stress on him. He had enough of that on his own. So, when she apologized, she meant it and she hoped he could tell.

"You do bring up a good point, though." He wagged a finger in the air. Taking in a deep breath before issuing a sharp sigh, he said, "Hold on here for a minute."

He looked at Arianna and then to Paisley, who was happily eating her dry cereal bit by bit.

"Think you guys will be okay in here for a minute? I just need to grab something from the office at the front of the house."

"Of course, we will. I never really inherited my aunt's gift with children but I'm not terrible with them and they seem to like me." Arianna didn't think this was the time to bring up the fact that she had some experience with kiddos. She wasn't ready to talk about Kiara.

KURT DASHED into the small home office off the living room. He retrieved his laptop from his desk and powered up. Cuzya stayed in the kitchen with Paisley. That dog rarely left her side. She'd curled up next to the highchair and was sleeping by the time Kurt came back into the room. He took a seat at the table, ignoring how right it looked for Arianna to be sitting across from him and so close to his daughter.

He told himself that it was nice to have someone in the house younger than a grandmother figure. Not that he didn't love Ms. Calaway because that couldn't be further from the truth. Getting through the past year wouldn't have been possible without her.

Talking Stacy into hiring a babysitter despite her protests had been one of his better moves. During her last month of pregnancy, all she'd wanted to do was rest. She'd argued against the idea of interviewing people when she wasn't her usual self.

Luckily, she came around and decided to start the process. Ms. Calaway was the seventh person interviewed and the only one Stacy fell in love with right away. There was something comforting about the fact his wife not only approved of Paisley's caregiver but had handpicked her.

But he missed companionship. That had been in short supply for him and he'd been devastated after losing his most beloved person in the world. He hadn't been around anyone who stirred his heart, reminding him it still beat in his chest or that thrill of attraction that had been dormant for so long. Those were the reasons he told himself it was good to be with Arianna and not because she was different or special even though that was the trick his mind was trying to play on him.

In fact, his mind was so made up that his pulse raced sitting near her and he had that same odd feeling that he hadn't had since he was a boy in high school. That nervousness, palm sweating feeling. That feeling of having a crush.

Despite waiting to have a family, he and Stacy had been together so long their relationship had morphed into something comfortable. There was something nice about having history with her. It was something he didn't realize he'd taken for granted until he lost her. But then that wasn't supposed to happen. They were supposed to have a lifetime together.

'Til death do us part' wasn't supposed to be this young with so much track ahead of them. There were so many memories yet to be made and the sense of loss was that rogue wave, always just out of sight but still there, waiting to take him under, toss him around, and drown him.

"What are you doing over there?" Arianna asked.

"Besides studying the screen?" He laughed because, Jesus, he needed to lighten the mood. He also wanted to show Arianna that he wasn't some intense guy she couldn't have a basic conversation with. "Looking for a home alarm installation company."

If she was going to be around for the next couple of hours while her aunt was being attended to, he wanted her to be able to relax around him. It was the least he could do after she'd been kind enough to step in and pitch in for her aunt.

"The two of you must be very close," he commented as he continued his search. It didn't take long to find one with the highest rating.

"You could say that."

Well, that wasn't much of an answer. Was she afraid to tell him more about herself? Or had he made her that uncomfortable around him? The thought made him feel pretty bad.

The circumstances in the last few hours were insane, but he wasn't exactly putting his best foot forward. It was a mistake he seemed to be making on a regular basis. One he needed to get a handle on if he was going to make a new friend.

A friend?

Yeah, because Kurt was really big on that. His hands were so full with the little one and running a successful business that he didn't prioritize social commitments. He considered people who worked for him friends. He was very friendly with his manager, Devin Sparks. Or, at least, he had been. Again, he almost laughed out loud. Being nice to someone who worked for him wasn't exactly the same as having someone to call up to go grab a beer with.

It wasn't until meeting Arianna that he thought he might even remotely be missing out on something. The feeling was strange.

"Could you hold on for a second?" he asked Arianna.

She seemed surprised by his politeness and that was another tell that he'd been quite a jerk so far. He'd find a way to make it up to her. Ms. Calaway deserved to have her niece treated better than he was.

"Yeah, go for it."

He picked up his cell and entered the number on the screen.

"The Best Alarm Company. How can I help you?" the chirpy voice asked.

"I need an alarm system installed in my house as soon as possible. How soon can you get someone out?"

"Um, let's see here. I have an opening next week. Can you do Tuesday?" the chirpy voice asked.

"What's your name?" he asked.

"Suzy."

"Well, Suzy, do you have anything sooner?" Kurt had built his storage supply business by being personal. Using first names was a step in that direction.

"I'm not seeing…no, sir. I don't."

"What if I told you money wasn't an object?" He'd tap into that McGannon fortune if it meant his daughter was safe. He didn't need to because he was successful in his own right. But there were no lengths to which he wouldn't go to ensure his daughter's safety.

"I can make some calls, sir. See if anyone would be willing to trade appointments. That's about the best I can do," Suzy said.

"Okay. I'll take it. Offer a thousand-dollar bonus to anyone willing to trade appointments." He could feel Arianna's eyes on him. He didn't normally make a show out of having money. This wasn't him flexing. This was necessity.

"Oh. Well. Um. I've never done that before but…yes…I'm happy to help. I'm sure that will ease some of the burden for someone. Can I get a credit card number to secure the offer?" Suzy wasn't stupid.

He rattled off his business account.

"Much appreciated, Suzy. If you can get someone to switch in the next forty-eight hours, I'm happy to extend the same bonus to you, as well."

"I'll see what I can do, sir."

"Kurt. Please. Call me Kurt."

"Will do, Kurt."

He didn't get a chance to say goodbye before the line went dead. Suzy was on it and he had a feeling she'd be calling him back pretty soon with the news he wanted to hear.

When he glanced up at Arianna, he was pretty sure that her jaw was about to hit the floor. As soon as their eyes made contact, she seemed to shake off the shock.

She refocused on Paisley, seeming that she was trying to divert the fact her cheeks had flushed. The rosy shade highlighted her violet eyes even more. Violet was his new favorite color.

"Wow." She said the word so low that he almost didn't hear. But he did.

"I'll get the front door fixed while I wait for a call back from the alarm company. Then, we'll figure out where we should stay tonight. I don't want you or your aunt here feeling vulnerable and I can't promise those men won't come back. It's safe to say they were chicken enough to wait for Cuzya and I to be long gone." The thought somebody had been most likely watching his house and waiting for him to leave sent an icy chill racing down his back. "How does that sound?"

Arianna was rocking her head. "I think that sounds good. No matter what my aunt says, I think she would take a couple of days off."

39

"Agreed." The thought of spending a couple of days in close quarters with Arianna sent a firebolt of electricity rocketing through him. It seemed a good time to remind himself that he was no longer a teenager with barely enough facial hair to warrant a shave. The hallmark of being a grown man was the ability to control his impulses. "I'll just grab some supplies from the garage and patch up that window until Henry can get here."

"That seems like a good idea. I'm okay here with Paisley. She seems to trust me enough to be alone with me." She glanced down at Cuzya. "And I seem to have approval from her to be inside the house."

Rhodesian ridgebacks were known for their protectiveness. Ever since Paisley had come home, Cuzya had been on double patrol.

"Yeah, I think you've won her over." He didn't have the heart to tell her that Cuzya seemed to have a sixth sense about people, or that anyone he trusted seemed to get a free pass.

Kurt walked into the garage and grabbed his toolbox along with a piece of plywood. He grabbed measuring tape before walking back inside to measure the size of plywood he would need to cut.

In his workshop, he made a quick cut on the wood before placing it on the door and hammering it in. "That should hold for the time being."

He'd feel a lot better about staying here with a fully loaded alarm system.

His ringtone sounded in the kitchen. He set the tools down and jogged over. The screen read, Levi McGannon.

The term not in the mood barely scratched the surface for Kurt. He figured he better take the man's call anyway.

5

"I heard what happened. Any idea who did this?" Levi started right in before Kurt had a chance at a greeting. The concern in Levi's voice struck a chord with Kurt.

"None. And I presume you're talking about what happened a few hours ago with my daughter. How did you know?" Kurt's curiosity was getting the best of him.

"It was my shift to sit with Dad and the sheriff happened to have stopped by when she got the call. She said she wanted each of us to stop by her office and talk to her at some point during the day. I pushed her for details and got out of her that someone tried to kidnap your daughter this morning," Levi said.

"My guess is something got stirred up from that article," Kurt admitted. His initial response to Levi had been defensive, so he cooled his jets. It seemed like distrust was the emotion he knew best. But Levi sounded genuine and Kurt could use a sounding board.

"Right. That would make sense. I wish the media would have left our personal business alone," Levi said.

"You didn't tell them?" Now, he really was curious. If not Levi, then who?

"Me? I realize that you don't actually know me very well, but you'll find that my brothers, cousins and I aren't exactly the types to run to the media every time something happens. We've grown up our whole lives exposed for everyone to judge and we're probably the last people who would call a reporter. But I have a sneaky suspicion that I know who in this house wouldn't have the same problem. My uncle.

Donny likes to stir up the pot, in case you haven't noticed. He's either bored or just wants to be a jerk. I have no idea which one and I won't make excuses for him." Levi's honesty formed a little bit of tentative trust between them for Kurt.

"That son of a—" Kurt glanced over at his little angel who was within earshot. Instead of finishing the thought, he blew out a frustrated sigh.

"I mean the thing is, what would he have to gain? I understand stirring up the pot but, in my experience, people don't do that unless they have something to gain," Kurt said.

"Listen, you are part of the family now and you should probably know this information. Donny was with Dad when he had his accident in the equipment room. Donny has been brought in for questioning several times since then and some of us are speculating that he's moving from witness to suspect. I can't tell you which camp he belongs in. All I can say is that I haven't trusted him since he spent his entire inheritance and then showed up with his hands out, asking for more. But I should probably keep my personal opinion to myself." Levi sounded resigned.

Kurt appreciated the man's honesty. And he also realized that Donny would have something to gain. "He wants a diversion."

"It's a distinct possibility as much as I don't like it or want it to be true," Levi stated on a frustrated-sounding sigh.

"If that man brought this down on my house..." Kurt reined himself in. He didn't need to be making a threat against a man who wasn't exactly popular.

"Believe me, we're all with you on that point."

It was a foreign feeling for someone else to have Kurt's back for a change. He wanted to trust Levi. His instincts said he could. But this guy had just found out that his father had to have cheated on his mother. He just found out that he wasn't the oldest McGannon despite seeming to have a lot of pride in the fact. And he just found out that his uncle was most likely stirring up the pot after being the only witness to Clive McGannon's accident.

Could Kurt trust Levi? Could he trust anyone? Could he lower his guard after what happened this morning?

"I don't know what you have going on at your house, but you and Paisley are welcome at the ranch. We have a guest house but there's plenty of room at the main house if you'd prefer staying there." Levi's offer was generous.

"I'm not sure if that's a good idea." Kurt was still trying to get his bearings with the fact he had a family beyond him and Paisley. This might not be the time to rush in.

"The only warning is that Uncle Donny has a room at the main house. I'd personally suggest taking me up on the offer of the guest house," Levi continued.

"Maybe later..."

"We can take this on your timetable. But you are part of this family now and it would be nice to get to know each other a little better. The best way to do that is by being under one roof or at the very least on the same property."

"Might be better to take this one step at a time," Kurt countered.

"Whatever you think is best. Just know that every McGannon here at the ranch is on your side," Levi said.

Somehow, Kurt doubted that. Don't get him wrong, he appreciated Levi for extending an olive branch. They had a long way to go toward trusting each other and he was really sure that not every McGannon felt the same way about having him and Paisley suddenly in the picture. Levi might be the oldest and he seemed to be a guy who stood by his word, but his brothers hadn't exactly reached out.

Kurt couldn't blame them. They'd been thrown for a loop as much as he had. They were a tightknit bunch from what he'd seen. Strong personalities. All with their own ideas. He'd had a conversation with A.J. in the hospital. A.J. was a decent guy, as well. Didn't mean he wanted Kurt in the family. And he didn't even remember the others' names. All he could remember so far was Levi, A.J., and Ryan. There were three others at the hospital suite that he'd probably been introduced to but had forgotten their names. Of course, there was one of him and a dozen of them, counting the cousins.

"Much appreciated," Kurt said.

He ended the call after exchanging goodbyes. Having a direct line to Levi McGannon might not be a terrible thing during this crisis. And he wasn't kidding. He did appreciate the fact Levi had reached out.

Lifting his gaze to Arianna, who was studying him, sent a jolt of electricity racing through him.

"It looks like you have things under control here with Paisley." He'd observed her quietly playing with his daughter, who seemed more than happy in her presence. "If it's okay with you, I'd like to disappear in my office for a little while. Work is piling up." A quick glance at his inbox revealed two hundred and twenty-seven unread messages.

Then there was his work cell phone, which had been buzzing pretty regularly during his conversation with Levi.

"We're good here. Right, Paisley?" She smiled at his little girl and Paisley practically cooed.

His heart nearly burst.

"Let's keep inside for this morning. Okay?" Again, he didn't want to think about how right it felt to have Arianna interacting so effortlessly with Paisley. Rather than let that get too far inside his head, he stood and picked up his laptop. With his free hand, he tucked his personal cell in his pocket and grabbed his work phone.

"You got it, chief. We'll stick to the living room and watch her favorite cartoons." Arianna saluted and the gesture made Paisley laugh.

"Help yourself to anything you need in the house. Anything in the fridge is all yours. I take it you know where her bedroom is and where the toys are?"

"If you could point me to the hallway leading to her bedroom, that would be great," she said.

Kurt nodded toward the stairwell off to the side of the living room. "Upstairs, first room on the right."

"Got it. Thanks." Seeing her hold his little girl's hand and watching Arianna's responses to her was another shot in the heart. "Have a good day at work. And don't worry about this little angel. We'll be fine. Plus, you're right here in the house if she needs you."

"Thanks." Kurt couldn't help himself. He glanced at the third finger on her left hand. He had no claim to her but the fact she wore no band and had no tan line still caused a flood of relief to wash over him. He chalked his reaction up to going too long without trying to date. Was he really that desperate? The first beautiful woman who walked inside his house and got along with his daughter sent his heart racing like he was some hormonal kid about to ask his crush to the high school dance.

He had that same sweaty-palm, heart-racing feeling now. And since that was about as productive as milking a lizard, he took that opportunity to leave the room.

It didn't take long to get settled in his office. Looking at his phone and seeing all the messages and new e-mails meant he'd be there a while.

Kurt needed to go back through his files. Any new client in the last thirty days would be worth taking a look at. Owning and operating a full-service storage business that offered various sizes with everything from warehouse space to those storage pods people left outside their houses when they were ready to move could lead to some potential issues. He always carefully vetted new clients just to make sure there was no funny business or offshore companies paying

45

invoices. Human trafficking along with arms dealing were always potential pitfalls in his line of work.

He took great measures to make sure his facilities and employees never got caught up in an illegal operation. The timing of the kidnapping attempt coinciding with the week he and the world found out he was a McGannon was most on his mind.

Plus, it didn't make sense to him the crime was related to his business. Why go for his daughter? Granted, his storage facilities were pretty unbreakable in terms of security. That didn't mean a real pro couldn't hack in or break in. Some might even see it as a challenge. But that would be theft. This involved more than somebody trying to steal contents. This had to be bigger.

Kurt also realized, while he was thinking on the business front, he needed to ask his manager to pull up any files of personal property that they'd seized in the past month. Holding onto someone's personal belongings for non-payment could definitely get sticky. It was worth looking into as a possibility for revenge.

His organization had grown and his manager, Devin, had been hiring a few new employees over the past six months.

Moving onto other lines of thinking, he had to consider there had to be straight-up gold diggers out there. Someone who'd read the article and wanted to snatch his daughter for ransom. He thought about the fact that Levi didn't trust their uncle. Donny had certainly stirred up the pot by reaching out to Kurt in the first place. The man's intentions seemed far from pure.

Anger fired through Kurt at the possibility he'd been played by Donny. Something happened to his daughter, maybe Donny was involved and wanted to pin it on one of the McGannons. He couldn't imagine that Donny would frame one of his own kids, so Kurt figured this could be a play on Levi and his brothers.

If Donny was involved in some type of illegal activity, like say, knocked Clive McGannon over the head with something and then left him there to die. Now, he could be moving on to set up one of Clive's boys. There were six of them, but he could try to take them out one by one and make it all look innocent.

It wasn't a quick solution, but it was a way he could gain control over the family's cattle ranch.

Kurt pushed up from his desk and started pacing. He couldn't ignore the fact that coming after his daughter was a very personal move. That brought his thinking back to the McGannons.

Sure, Levi had reached out. What about the others?

The thought of going to the ranch didn't seem so bad after all. Maybe he didn't want to stay there on the property or get too comfortable. He did want to look each one of his new family members in the eyes.

Kurt regarded himself as an excellent judge of character and he was convinced that if he looked someone in the eyes who wanted to hurt him or Paisley, he'd know it. There'd been countless times, especially when his business was new, that he'd had to make the call on whether or not he could trust someone. His instincts had always been spot-on.

No matter what, he needed to call Devin in and have a sit down. Considering Kurt's personal life had become news fodder, he wanted his top manager to hear the news about the kidnapping attempt firsthand from him.

Kurt picked up his phone and fired off a text, requesting Devin to stop by. The response came a few seconds later. Devin was on his way. About the same time, a knock sounded at the door.

Pushing up to standing, Kurt came around his desk in a heartbeat. He made his way over to the front door, and then opened it for Henry.

"What do we have here?" Henry asked. He was already examining the piece of plywood that Kurt had placed to cover the broken windowpane.

"Yeah, it got broken." Kurt was hesitant to give too many details. Not because he didn't trust Henry, but Kurt didn't open up to many people about the details of his private life. He didn't want a lot of questions.

Devin deserved to know what was going on. Kurt interacted with his manager on a daily basis and he was the closest thing Kurt had to a friend.

"Teenagers," Henry said under his breath and Kurt didn't correct the man.

He wished. "Think you can get that fixed up for me?"

"Does a chicken lay eggs?" Henry chuckled at his own joke. He was tall with a full head of gray hair. Despite being in his late sixties and thin, he was strong. His disposition made Kurt think the man fit behind a podium, giving a lecture on physics to eager college students. With a pencil tucked behind his ear, and hair that looked like it hadn't seen a comb in days, Henry had the whole absent-minded professor demeanor down.

"I imagine they do." Kurt chuckled along with Henry. Kurt was keenly aware that Arianna had moved into the living room with Paisley. She'd set up a blanket on the floor with some toys. She had cartoons playing on the TV and was helping Paisley play with the toys scattered on the blanket.

It was another scene that hit him square in the chest.

6

Kurt's *personal cell buzzed in his pocket. He fished it out and*

checked the screen before glancing at Arianna. The name on his phone read, Raul.

"Henry, I need to take this one. You got this?" he asked.

"Has a bird got wings?" The repairman was already fixated on the door as he laughed at his second joke. His big red toolbox was already sitting on the porch and he was already digging deep into his tool belt.

Kurt answered the call.

"Good news on Bea," Raul started right in. "She's going to be fine. The doctors want to keep her here overnight for observation but it's just a precaution. They fully expect to release her in the morning."

"That's really good to hear," Kurt said.

"I thought you'd want to know," Raul confirmed. "She twisted her ankle up pretty well. The doctor was worried there might be a break based on the swelling, but the X-ray was good, so he figures it's a hairline fracture. She'll need to be off her feet for a few days but then she'll be good as new."

"She can take all the time she needs to heal. There's no rush on my end. I can cover for her here as long as she needs." All Kurt cared about was Ms. Calaway's health. He would figure out a plan to cover Paisley. The honest truth was that he had no intention of letting his little girl out of his sight.

"I had to come into the hallway to call you because she wanted to take over the call." The lightness in Raul's tone was welcomed. It meant he was relaxed and calm, which in turn meant that Ms. Calaway was doing great. "The doctor gave her some medication once he ruled out a head injury and he wants her to get some rest. So, I had to slip out to tell you."

Raul's affection for Ms. Calaway came through clearly in his tone.

"Thank you for the update. That is really great news. Tell Ms. Calaway not to worry about coming to work anytime soon. Her job is here when she's ready."

"She's already trying to figure out a way to be released from here so she can come back to work tomorrow," he said.

"Not a chance. It's her job to stay put until she heals up her injuries. I don't care how long that takes." Kurt meant every word. He also knew full well how stubborn his babysitter could be. She would also see being home healing as abandoning him and he needed to set the record straight.

"I'll tell her what you said, but you know Bea," Raul said. Apparently, Kurt's neighbor knew 'Bea' fairly well and for the first time Kurt wondered if something special was brewing between the two of them.

There must be something in the air, he thought, as he looked at Arianna. It was the only explanation for him to allow an attraction like the one he felt for her to take over his thoughts to this degree.

Setting those thoughts aside, he ended the call with Raul and moved to where she sat on the blanket, legs folded.

"That was Raul?" she immediately asked. Hope written all over her face.

"Yes. He says your aunt is going to be fine," he relayed the rest of the message.

"I don't mind stepping in for her while she heals. If she knows I'm here and Paisley is covered, she might actually stay home and rest that ankle," she said.

He nodded.

It was all kinds of wrong to want Arianna to stay. He certainly didn't want it at the expense of Ms. Calaway's health. And yet, he liked the idea of her being around.

"You don't have work to go to?" He regretted the question when she dipped her head down, chin to chest before giving a quick shake. He'd no doubt hit a touchy subject and had no plans to look a gift horse in the mouth. Besides, he wanted to get to know Arianna better, telling himself that it was for Paisley's sake. He tried to convince himself that he wanted to know who would be taking care of his daughter.

"That should about do it." Henry's voice cut through their conversation.

Kurt turned around to see a perfect fix on the glass. Henry opened and closed the door a couple of times.

"Excellent," he said. "Now, onto the lock."

Henry shot a quizzical look at Kurt, like he was putting two-and-two together, realizing this was more than just about a teenager who threw a rock at a window and then took off.

Thankfully, Henry didn't ask despite his arched brow. He shook his head like he was shaking off the questions forming in his mind before going right back to work. He picked up a flathead screwdriver and a lock mechanism.

Kurt wanted to say something to smooth things over with Arianna. He wanted to find a way to tell her that her work situation didn't matter. He wanted to find the words to say that he wanted her to stay with him and Paisley until her aunt was well enough to come back to work.

Since no magic words came, he settled on, "Hey, I'm glad that you're here. I'm not sure what I would've done without you."

The smile his words brought to her face could light a dark room. She didn't look up at him when she said, "I'm happy to be here."

BEING with Paisley and Kurt was dangerous to Arianna's heart. It was clear the single dad loved his daughter. It was also very sweet and touched her more than she wanted to allow. She sat up a little straighter and reminded herself that she was there to pitch in for her beloved aunt, not fall for the guy with the adorable daughter.

It was a little too easy to think about how good the scruff on his chin would feel against her neck as he kissed his way down...

Nice, Ari. Way to keep those emotions in check.

Arianna forced her gaze away from the handsome stranger. Yes, stranger. It didn't matter how comfortable she felt with Kurt Johnson, he was still a stranger. She didn't know him from Adam.

And it was easy to forget that fact when she was staring into those dark eyes of his—eyes that promised a whole lot of sinning on Sundays.

So, she refocused on Paisley.

"She's a sweetheart."

"Yeah. I feel like I got lucky with her. She's always been an easy baby. I used to joke that she was born with a smile on her face." There was a wistful quality to his voice that captivated her. It was easy to sense his loss. Was it Paisley's mother?

Oh, that had to be it. Had he lost his wife after the birth of this beautiful little girl? Arianna had checked his ring finger earlier and detected a faint tan line but no gold band. Was it because his wife had died?

Well, her heart really was in trouble now as well as pretty much every other part of her because she felt an undeniable pull to Kurt despite her best efforts to shut it down. There was something in his eyes, something so broken that seemed to fit the broken parts in her. Arianna had never felt such a powerful connection with anyone in her past.

"Hello, boss," an unfamiliar male voice coming from the doorway stopped her mid-stare.

"DEVIN, COME IN," Kurt said to his manager. At twenty-seven, he reminded Kurt so much of himself at that age and that entrepreneurial spark was the reason Devin had the responsibility of being Kurt's top guy in the field. His manager had earned an associate degree in business and had now been with Kurt for three years. He got the job by showing up for an open interview and then volunteering to run Kurt's errands for free on a trial basis.

The guy had been hungry to prove himself and worked hard. Upfront, he admitted to having a juvenile record, now sealed, but said he got his life on track. Evidence of his turnaround was impressive.

"All right." Devin stepped inside and his gaze darted around, searching for something...someone?

Kurt hadn't mentioned the attempted kidnapping, so it couldn't be the reason. He glanced one last time at Arianna, holding the stare for a second too long. His heart clenched and his stomach twisted. To say a moment had just happened between them—was still happening between them—was the understatement of the day. The crazy pull he felt toward her caught him off guard. The earth tilted on its axis as a *groundswell swept over him and through him. The feeling was unlike any other. He'd never felt anything this remarkable or strong with Stacy. He chalked it up to the fact the two of them had been together since high school. A crush had turned into something stronger and carried them through. And it didn't seem fair to put what he felt with Arianna in the same category. Rather than get inside his head about it, Kurt shook Devin's outstretched hand.*

"We can talk in my office," Kurt said.

Devin kept his head down and his focus on his shoes as he walked by the living room on his way to Kurt's office. Paisley was way too into the cartoon playing and the toy she was cramming in her mouth, to acknowledge anyone at the moment.

The office was right off the living room. Double French doors wouldn't give them a ton of privacy, but Kurt closed them behind Devin anyway to muffle the cartoon sound from the adjacent room.

"Everything okay?" Devin asked after seeming to study Kurt for a long moment.

Kurt took a seat at his desk. "Yeah. No. Bad morning." He leveled his gaze at his employee. "You'll probably hear the news now that my life seems to be front page worthy and I wanted you to hear from me first."

"That doesn't sound good." Devin sat a little straighter. He placed the flats of his palms on top of his thighs. His right foot tapped double time on the wood flooring. "Does this have anything to do with Henry installing a new lock at the front door?"

"As a matter of fact, it does," Kurt admitted. "Someone broke in this morning while Cuzya and I were on a run."

"Jesus, Kurt. Is everyone okay?" He glanced around. "Where's Ms. Calaway?"

"In the hospital but she'll recover," Kurt said on a sharp sigh. He was frustrated with himself for not being here when the kidnapper broke in.

"Is that why there's a stranger in the next room with Paisley?" Devin continued. His concern was evident in his tone. He was more like family than employee.

"Arianna is Ms. Calaway's niece."

"Oh." Devin rocked his head and that foot tapped even more. Keep it up and he'd become a tap dancer. "I got it. She's pinch-hitting for her aunt. But that must've been some kind of accident if she's in the hospital."

"She took a turn on her ankle and it's fractured. She'll be released tomorrow." Kurt studied his employee as Devin wiped his hand across his mouth. "Everything okay?"

"Yes, well, you know how it is. Pregnant wife at home and..." Devin seemed to catch himself. He shot an apologetic look at Kurt.

"It's okay. You can talk about your pregnant wife around me," Kurt reassured. The closer his wife got to her due date, the more stressed Devin seemed to be getting. Par for the course for a first-time parent.

Devin compressed his lips despite nodding. Kurt was used to guys being uncomfortable bringing up their spouses in front of him.

"You called the cops, right?" Devin asked and Kurt noticed the pivot in conversation.

"Yes," Kurt said.

"Cops catch the guys?"

"Nope. No idea who broke in because they weren't looking to steal jewelry or electronics. They came for Paisley."

The shock and horror on Devin's face would be etched in Kurt's memory for a long time. It mirrored his own emotions when he'd gotten the call from his neighbor about the break-in.

"Why? Who would do such a thing to your little girl?" he asked and then it seemed to dawn on him. "The new brothers you have? Are they responsible?" Devin pushed to standing and started pacing in the small space.

"Not that I know of." Although Kurt had every intention of looking each one in the eye at some point in the very near future.

"Then who?"

Kurt leaned forward, propping his elbows against his desk. "Between you and me, I think this is personal. The cops are working with Sheriff Justice of Cattle Cove." He realized Devin would have no idea where that was. "The town where the McGannons live."

"Are they cooperating?"

Kurt nodded.

"Does this have anything to do with that article?" Devin asked.

"Good question," Kurt said. "I'm trying to cover every base here and I might be barking up the wrong tree. But I'd rather be wrong than stupid. Can I get a report of all the new clients and any new hires going back the last six months and a list of names of recent property seizures?"

"You got it, Kurt." Devin's eyes were wide as he reclaimed his seat. "You think it's possible someone is trying to get back at you because of something related to work?"

"I'm considering every possibility when it comes to someone threatening my little girl," he admitted.

"That's a good point. I won't argue there." Devin shifted his weight.

"Has there been anything suspicious going on at the office?" Kurt asked.

"Not really. Nothing of this magnitude. I've been handling something that I didn't want to trouble you with. Someone was using one of our containers for trafficking purposes. I opened up a container…and let's just leave it at the fact no one survived," he said. "They were young. Some as little as twelve years old if I had to guess."

"When did this happen?" Kurt's heart practically ripped from his chest. He went to great lengths to ensure his company was used for legal purposes only. The idea a criminal could slip past their controls and the senseless loss of life sent white-hot anger racing through him.

"I intercepted the container three days ago and immediately reported it to authorities. Like always. It was going to be in my report this week. I just haven't gotten around to putting it on paper yet," he admitted, clasping his hands together.

Finding illegal substances and sadly sometimes people in one of their containers wasn't exactly new even though it was rare because they had a system of vetting out criminals. "Are you doing okay with everything you have going on at home?"

"This one got to me." He shivered. "Maybe it was the age of the victims. You know, Carla's due soon and I can't help but think about what I would do if something happened to my little girl after she's born. I think different now that I'm going to be a dad. I'm more concerned with other people's kids than I ever have been."

Kurt commiserated with the sentiment. Human trafficking was right up there on a list of parent's worst nightmares. But so was a child being abducted from home.

"You know how these things usually work," Devin continued, getting up to pace again.

"No one is ever convicted, and the paperwork trail is soft," Kurt said.

"Yeah, except this trail leads back to a judge in Travis County." Devin stopped behind the chair he'd been sitting in and gripped the back of it.

"A powerful man in a job he wouldn't want to lose." This didn't sound good at all. It was bad enough when a person committed a crime, but someone sworn to protect people was the worst of low.

"Exactly. But what's bugging me is why would the paperwork lead back to him? Wouldn't a judge be more careful?"

Two words came to Kurt. "Set up."

7

K urt pulled out the officer's card from earlier and set it on the desk. This information might have no connection to what happened at his house this morning, but he wasn't willing to risk it. He picked up his cell phone next and made the call.

"Officer Forth, this is Kurt Johnson. You were here at my home a little—"

"Yes, sir. What can I do for you?" the officer asked.

"First off, my employee is here, and he just gave me news that I thought you should know. Can I put the call on speaker?" Kurt asked.

"Okay by me."

Kurt set the phone down and introduced Devin. After greetings, Devin filled the officer in.

"I'll turn this over to the detective being assigned to the case," Officer Forth said.

"I didn't have a name when I gave my statement to law enforcement," Devin admitted.

"But you do now?"

"Yes, sir." Devin gripped the chair tighter. "Judge McCann."

The officer issued a sharp sigh. "And you have evidence to prove the judge is involved?"

"I have a trail that leads to him," Devin corrected.

"We suspect that it's too easy and someone might be trying to set up the judge," Kurt interjected. He glanced into the living room and caught a glimpse of Paisley and Arianna. The sight of the two of them, together, warmed him in places that had been dead this year. She threatened to wake up his heart and make him think he might not spend the rest of his life alone. Meeting someone special wasn't something he considered possible or welcome.

"I have files to turn over as evidence," Devin said.

"Electronic?"

"Yes, sir."

"Can I get those on a flash drive?" Officer Forth asked. "I'd also like for you to bring in the device those files are stored on."

"They're in the cloud. We don't keep them on individual computers," Kurt stated.

"Right. Then, I'll swing by and get the flash drive from you once I close out the call I'm currently on," Officer Forth said.

"Thank you, sir," Devin said.

"Am I coming by your house, Mr. Johnson, or is there a secondary location?"

Kurt looked to Devin, who rattled off the business address.

"I can swing by there now. I need to get back to work anyway," Devin said, twisting his hands together. He was on edge. What he was dealing with was big and there were a lot of implications.

They finished up the details and ended the call with the officer. With Carla's due date looming, Devin had stress coming at him on all fronts.

The guy needed a break and Kurt had every intention of coming up with a plan. In the foreseeable future, his full attention would be on keeping Paisley safe. But as soon as the bastards who'd broken into his home and tried to snatch her were locked behind bars, he had every intention of taking over some of Devin's load in the final few weeks of his wife's pregnancy.

"You got everything covered here?" Devin asked.

"Yes. Lock is getting fixed. Alarm company is trying to work out an appointment for in the morning," Kurt said.

Kurt showed Devin out and he saw the way Devin glanced at Paisley. Regret? Concern?

Devin seemed on the brink of stress. Kurt knew how much Devin cared about Paisley. He'd been around from day one and had been shouldering most of the business burden while Kurt navigated those early days with his newborn.

Henry opened the door for Devin on his way out. The two exchanged pleasantries and Kurt could scarcely tear his gaze away from Arianna with his daughter.

"All done," Henry said, handing over a new set of keys as Kurt's cell buzzed—a call back from the alarm company.

He said a quick goodbye to Devin, asked Henry to hold tight for a minute, and then answered the call on his personal cell.

"This is Kurt."

"Sir, I'm happy to be able to tell you that I can book an appointment for you first thing in the morning. It's early...at seven o'clock. Does that work for your schedule?" Suzy also seemed pleased with herself. Kurt was two for three this morning, but he'd work on getting Devin the help he needed.

"Sounds like a plan." He rattled off his address for the appointment and reminded her about the bonuses. "I'll okay the charges. I appreciate all your help on this."

"Not a problem, sir. Let me know if there's anything else that I can help you with," she chirped. He had to give it to her, she was perky.

They ended the call as Kurt signed off on Henry's work. Paisley had settled into Arianna's lap and had fallen asleep. She absently stroked the little girl's hair and his heart practically burst.

A conversation needed to happen with Arianna about the possibility of her sticking around for a few days while her aunt healed. If he had someone set up to take care of Paisley who Ms. Calaway trusted, he had a much better chance of convincing her to keep some weight off that fracture and allowing herself some time to get better.

He could continue to run his business from home temporarily, like he had been. Getting back into the office to relieve Devin jumped up the priority scale.

Kurt locked the door and the new deadbolt with the keys that Henry had provided. He pocketed them. His back door should be fine. It had a special bolt-style lock, but his front door had obviously been his most vulnerable point. As he walked back inside his office, the thought struck that the person could come back. Would he?

He was obviously a coward. And opportunistic.

Kurt considered whether or not the kidnapping could have been orchestrated by a professional as he reclaimed his seat at his desk. He scooted his chair over, close enough to keep one eye on the living room. Not that he didn't trust Arianna. Clearly, he trusted her with his life. But because he needed the ability to keep one eye on his little girl. He'd spent far too much time in the last year afraid something might happen to take her away from him, too.

He just needed to be able to look up from his work and see that she was there and safe. It would take a while to shake off the stress from such a close call.

Kurt looked through file after file. There was no sign of anything out of the ordinary on the paperwork. The name, Thomas McCann, had been linked to a file through a credit card payment. That was where the trail began and ended.

The rest of the afternoon was spent working in his office. He barely came up for air and when he did, he found a sandwich had been made and put in the fridge for him. He thanked Arianna and ate at his desk. Dinner came and went.

Arianna knocked on the office door. He blinked blurry eyes at her, blurry from staring at the screen for too long and she was a welcomed sight.

"Sorry to interrupt. Thought you might want to give her a goodnight kiss before I take her up to bed." Arianna had Paisley on her hip.

"That's the best idea I've heard all day," he said with a smile. "You don't have to apologize for stopping by. There's literally nothing more important in my world than this little bean right here." He stood up and walked over to his girl, taking note of the temperature change as he stood close to Arianna.

He had to give it to her. He hadn't had these feelings in longer than he could remember, and no amount of teen hormone-fueled crushes came anywhere near this.

The last twelve months amounted to a blur of diapers and exhaustion, all while learning accounting on the fly, which had been the equivalent of drinking from a fire hose.

"Thank you for everything you're doing for her and for me," he said. "You can't know how much I appreciate you being here." He meant every word. He wasn't sure what he would've done without her there to help out with Paisley and give his daughter some sense of normalcy while he tried to figure out what was going on. Investigations took time and he knew the longer it took to get a trail, the less likely an arrest would be. Cold cases were called 'cold' for a reason and based on some articles he'd read a long time ago a cold trail wasn't a good trail. So, anything he could do to speed things along would help investigators.

"You're welcome. She's a sweet girl." She said it like it was nothing but her being there meant everything to Kurt. "I'm really happy to help out."

She started walking over and he met her halfway. He gave his daughter a kiss.

"Night-night, Dada." That smile melted his heart every time. It had the power to dissolve a brutal day—the kind that normally would've wiped him out. Somehow, he found the reserves to hold

Paisley another hour when his arms felt like they might fall off when she didn't want to go to bed. That kid had his heart in her tiny little hand.

The two disappeared after a quick kiss. The draw toward Arianna was another matter. It was the strongest he'd felt. Don't get him wrong, he'd loved his wife. They'd met in high school and were best friends. Obviously, they'd planned to have a long life together.

The plan had always been for him to work his tail off while Stacy finished school. He'd put his head down in order to build a business so that one day when they had a child, he could step back a little bit from the reins. He'd been grooming Devin for the past couple of years to be able to take on more responsibility.

And then, Stacy died just as they were starting their real plan. Granted, she'd turned up pregnant a couple of years before they were ready on the career front, but he never once saw the pregnancy as an inconvenience. Life happened. He never looked at Paisley as anything more than an unexpected gift, as welcome as Christmas in July after a hard summer.

So, rather than wait until the exact perfect time, they'd gone for it. His wife had decided she wanted to be a full-time mother and he supported her decision a hundred percent. If she wanted to work, he would've supported that, too.

She'd handled the company's website and helped him with the books from day one, so he was still trying to play catch up there in the past year. She'd asked him if he would consider hiring an accountant once the baby came and he'd agreed.

Being an entrepreneur, he'd always watched cost and worried about spending. It was part of the formula that had made him successful at a young age. But it also caused him to keep tight hold on the reins and, sometimes, not spend when he should. He was a work in progress on that one.

The human trafficking news hit him hard. The storage request shouldn't have slipped past the gates. Guilt was a bucket of ice water poured over his head. He'd been in a fog after losing his wife and caring for a newborn. But that stopped now. He took full responsibility for the slip in his security. He needed to find a way to better vet people to make sure this thing didn't slip through a crack. He was grateful for the spot check that saved them. He also needed to go into the office and get more facetime with his employees.

Working from home had been a godsend with a new baby and babysitter he didn't know from Adam. But once this situation was handled, and it would be, he needed to show his face more often at the office.

Now, more than ever, he needed his business to be a success. He couldn't afford heat from government officials if slips in security let traffickers use his locations.

There were a lot of things in his life that the time was coming to move forward. It wasn't good for him or Paisley to linger in the past and only focus on what could have been or what was supposed to have been. He could admit to not really rocking it out on the work front.

Kurt glanced at the clock. He'd been staring at the screen so long that his eyes were blurry. It was just past ten o'clock and he wanted to check on his daughter while she slept. He also wanted to make sure Arianna had everything she needed to be comfortable. He could offer her a laptop or something so she could at least watch movies or do whatever she did to wind down.

He logged off his computer and shut it down. Besides, he needed to get upstairs and ask Arianna if she'd heard from her aunt. They needed to come up with a plan to keep Ms. Calaway from overdoing it and hurting herself even more.

Taking the stairs two at a clip, his heart rate doubled with every hop. His pulse started racing and his palms got sweaty. He shook it off and kept going. As he reached the top of the stairs, he was suddenly concerned that Arianna might already be asleep. He really did want to talk to her and maybe put her at ease about staying at his home. As much as she was a stranger to him, the reverse was true. She didn't know him from Adam, and he wanted to be able to put any fears she might have about him or the situation at ease.

It helped that he had the endorsement from her aunt, someone she was obviously very close to and loved very much. He'd heard Ms. Calaway talk about her niece all the time and was a little bit embarrassed that he just assumed she was a little girl. In fact, he knew embarrassingly little about his babysitter's life.

She'd been an angel, showing up in his darkest days and helping him ride out the apex of his grief. She'd always been a little overprotective over him and Paisley because she'd been on the front line since day one. She'd had a front row seat to his anguish.

He softly knocked on the door before stepping over the rail meant to stop Paisley from wondering out of her room and into the stairwell where she could fall down the stairs. Her room had a Jack and Jill bath and another bedroom was on the other side of it. Ms. Calaway said she was a light sleeper and always left the doors open between rooms.

Suddenly, he felt awkward in his own home. Like he was invading Arianna's privacy. On second thought, she might be asleep, and he didn't think it was right to disturb her. He'd check on his daughter and head back downstairs.

The lights were low in Paisley's room. He walked over to her crib before placing both hands on the railing. He watched as her chest raised and fell. He'd lost track of how many times he'd done the same thing. Standing at her bedside. Counting her breaths. Making sure she was still breathing.

Kurt could almost feel the moment Arianna walked into the room. He could feel the air change, and his heart warm a little bit more. It was a foreign feeling for him for somebody to have an impact on him just by walking into the room. He hadn't had that in a very long time.

Even in his last year with Stacy, everything had been different. He expected that things would have gotten back to normal at some point. They had to, right?

He chalked it up to the changes that come with the territory. Not that it hadn't freaked him out at first when she seemed to get upset for no reason. Her mood swings were the stuff of legend. She complained about him working all the time and not being there for her despite telling him to earn as much as he could to support their baby. Those complaints stung the most now in part because they were true. He had put his head down and worked extra during her pregnancy. At the time, he convinced himself that he was making sure she could stay home once the baby came.

Was that true?

8

K urt questioned himself every day after losing her. Guilt was a near-constant companion. He regretted not closing the office door at five o'clock and watching that movie she wanted to see with him.

He thought he had time. That was the real kicker. No one knew exactly how much time they had or what unexpected event would happen the next day that would change the trajectory of their life.

Arianna cleared her throat. He turned his head to the side to acknowledge her presence. She joined him at the crib and a jolt of electricity shot through him when their shoulders grazed. She pulled back quickly and he wondered if she felt that same sudden shock of awareness.

The two of them stood there, looking down at the little miracle that was Paisley. He loved watching her sleep. She looked so…peaceful.

After a few minutes, he nodded toward the other room. Arianna took the lead, walking through the Jack and Jill and into her aunt's room. There was a full-sized bed against one wall and probably the most comfortable overstuffed chair in the corner. Next to it was a table that had a stack of books on top. There were more stacked on the floor, next to it. Ms. Calaway liked to read before bed.

Arianna took a seat in the big chair. Kurt sat on the floor, using the bed as back support.

The lights were dim except for a reading light that was on the book stand. It looked like Arianna followed in her aunt's footsteps with her love of reading.

Kurt extended his arms, resting his elbows on his bent knees. "I want to make sure you know how much I appreciate you being here, for one. You didn't have to step in for your aunt but I'm sure glad you did."

"I would do pretty much anything for my aunt." There was so much sincerity in her tone. He had no doubt she meant every word. "Aunt Bea is an amazing person."

They both seemed to agree on that. "I thought maybe if you were up for talking for a little while that we could get to know each other better. Staying in a stranger's house can sometimes feel awkward and I thought it might be easier if you got to know me a little better."

She was nodding her head and he took that as a sign to continue.

"Well, you already know my name is Kurt Johnson, although, I just found out that it probably should be McGannon." He chuckled.

"Of the McGannons of Texas?" She blinked a few times.

"The very ones," he admitted.

"Do you think that could be the reason behind what happened this morning?"

"I can't rule it out as much as I'd like to, but there is a scenario that says someone wanted to take my daughter for ransom money now that it's publicly known that I'm tied to the wealthy family." He blew out a frustrated breath. "The truth is that I don't even know how I feel about being a McGannon. I don't feel like one. I still feel like myself. Not much has changed, and I don't want their money."

"I get it. It's good to have a family. I'm guessing Paisley's mom—"

"She died during childbirth." He went ahead and got that out there. He was surprised that Ms. Calaway hadn't already told her and yet the fact she protected details about his life warmed him from the inside out.

"Oh, Kurt. I'm so sorry. I can't even imagine what that must have been like for you to lose the one woman you'd planned to spend the rest of your life with. That's so unfair." Her compassion was balm to the broken pieces of his soul.

"I'm surprised your aunt didn't tell you." All he could do was thank Arianna for her kindness.

"My aunt is protective of the people she cares about. You'll never find someone who has your back more than Aunt Bea." She shrugged as more of that compassion came through in her tone. "She probably didn't think it was her story to tell."

"I understand that thinking," he said, figuring he could fill in a few details for Arianna. "She…Stacy…that was her name…"

"Pretty name," Arianna said.

"She was the one who did most of the interviewing when I finally convinced her to hire help for the baby. We figured she was the one who would be interacting with the babysitter the most between the two of us. I remember the day she interviewed your aunt. I could have sworn up until meeting her that my wife was sabotaging interviews." He chuckled at the memory. It would have been just like Stacy to pull something like that. Pretend to go along with the plan while secretly not following the plan at all. "But the sparkle in her eye when she told me about your aunt was undeniable. I told her to go with her instincts and offer the job. Anyone who could break through Stacy's walls in one interview had to be impressive."

"Your wife sounds like someone who knew what she wanted when she saw it," Arianna said.

He nodded. That was one way of looking at it. "Your aunt has been a godsend to me and Paisley for the past year."

"I can tell that you're pretty special to my aunt," she admitted. "She gossips about people she doesn't like."

Arianna laughed and it was about the most musical thing he'd heard. Just like a good riff, her voice traveled all over him.

Kurt took in a long, slow breath, trying to calm his racing pulse. He didn't necessarily think his body's reaction to Arianna was a bad *thing. To him, it just proved that he still had a beating heart in his chest. That had to be a good sign because there were times in this past year that it hurt so much, he had to shut it down to survive. And then he just forgot to flip the switch again and allow anyone in his life.*

Paisley was the exception. He lived for that child. And now he had the possibility to give her a real family.

"We were talking about my new family before. Finding out that I have all these siblings and cousins that I never knew about...I have mixed feelings..."

"Yeah? I doubt you'd be human if you didn't," she said before looking at him with the most beautiful eyes. Even in the dim light, he could see their sparkle. "I mean, it's about having a family, right?"

"Not so much for me. I've always thought that I was pretty okay on my own." He nodded toward Paisley's room. "It's mainly for her. I want her to have more than just me."

"I understand completely. I'm guessing that your mom is..."

"Gone. I lost her a few years back. It became me and Stacy against the world at a young age. She had family but they never really talked to her. Her parents divorced when she was still in high school and it was bad. She stayed with her mom and everything was okay for a little while until her mom remarried and decided to move out of the country. They basically had a social media relationship from that point on. Meaning, occasionally her mother would post a new picture of her and her husband in their new life overseas, but for all intents and purposes, she and her mother lost contact. It was one of the many reasons Stacy had said she would never get divorced. She didn't care what happened in a marriage, she'd find a way to make it work. Looking back, I can see that she wanted a sense of family as much as I did. It bonded us and made us closer." Was it strange that he didn't describe his wife as the great love of his life?

Those weren't the words that came to him when he thought about her. He thought about things like companion, history, and best friend.

"We started dating sophomore year in high school and were together ever since."

ARIANNA WATCHED Kurt as he spoke about the woman he'd intended to spend the rest of his life with. There was so much reverence in his voice. It struck her in a deep place. She could only wonder what it would be like to have someone love her to that degree. Her ex-boyfriend had clearly loved himself more and if she was being honest, she had dated a string of men who put themselves first, their needs first. But then she'd always kind of kept the door open in a relationship. She never walked fully into a room, always leaving one eye on the exit.

As much as she liked the idea of finding that one person, she could be honest enough to admit that there was a definite pattern to her dating. She sure wouldn't have been mature enough in high school to know what she wanted for the rest of her life.

"It's kind of a beautiful thing that you guys stayed together and were building a family. I think I read somewhere that a really small number of people who meet and marry in high school actually go the distance. It seems like you guys would have made it," she said.

Kurt nodded. It was a good thing overall for a relationship to stick together. Strangely, she didn't like the thought of him being with someone else. So, clearly, she was being very successful reining in her attraction to him.

Just being in the same room with him, she could feel his presence like she'd never felt anyone in a room before. She also was keenly aware of the fact that even if he felt the same draw, it could never go anywhere.

"You must've loved your wife very much." She also realized any feelings she had for Kurt, and the attraction was strong, she would be fighting an uphill battle with a memory...a ghost...and no one could compete with that, no matter how strong the attraction between them.

What was she even thinking? It wasn't like Kurt Johnson or McGannon or whatever his last name ended up being was asking her out or evaluating being in a relationship with her. Not to mention the fact she wasn't in the market to date another single dad. Period. Been there. Done that. Got the emotional scars to prove it.

"I did. Still do. And I see so much of her in our daughter. There are times when I feel like she's still with us."

"She is. I mean, like you said, she will always be part of your daughter. What you guys had...what you were able to create out of the love you had for each other is sleeping in the next room and that's a pretty beautiful thing, despite the sadness that comes with losing somebody you love, and I can only imagine how horrible that must be. I can't say that I've experienced anything remotely close to that kind of love." Arianna had to hold her breath for a moment to stem the emotion threatening to spill over. She was almost thirty years old and was quite certain that she could honestly in her heart of hearts say that she had never been loved by anyone that much. That soul-deep need to be with just one person had never existed in her life.

And the funniest thing was that despite feeling a hole in her chest for longer than she cared to remember, she would never have been able to put into words the thing that was missing in her life until now.

"You know that saying, It's better to have loved and lost than never to have loved at all?" Kurt asked after a thoughtful pause.

"Yeah, I've heard it."

"I wonder about it some days. It's getting easier with time to forget her despite spending half my life with her. It's those little things that are disappearing. And I have no memories of her with Paisley, who is my life now. People describe this phase as closing a chapter in one life and opening a new one. It's more like there was this life in a totally different universe and then I woke up one morning to find everything I knew or thought or made sense to me was gone. And then...don't get me wrong, Paisley is my heart...but I'm left with this whole new experience that I'm never going to share with that person, and I don't have a lot of time to adjust. Missing the one you love while caring for this fragile little thing...I was afraid I might break her at first. She was just this tiny thing that I was afraid to hold. Until your aunt showed me, little by little, the right way to hold her and then change a diaper. Day by day we go through it in the alternate universe we were handed. You know?"

She nodded. Even though she couldn't fathom losing her life partner. "It takes a lot of courage to pick up the pieces after life knocks you down."

His warm smile lit a bunch of tiny little fires inside her. He was devastatingly handsome when he smiled.

"I can't begin to understand what you've been through," she admitted. Losing her mother wasn't quite the same thing. "I can only imagine...I can't say that I've gone through anything that can compare to losing a spouse. The only thing worse would be losing a child."

"That one...I can't even think about it." He issued a sharp sigh before turning the tables on her. "So, have you always been close to your aunt?"

"Not when I was really little. I didn't know her. My mom had a hard time being a single parent. Or, just taking care of me. I'm not sure which. She always needed someone in her life...a man. I had a lot of," she made air quotes with her fingers, "uncles. If you know what I mean."

He looked at her like he was capable of seeing right through her. Having that connection was oddly comforting. She didn't normally talk about things so personal, and yet with Kurt, it felt like the most natural thing. Maybe it was the broken side of him connecting with the broken side of her. She didn't know or care. This was the first time she actually wanted to talk to someone about her past.

"I got bounced around. Some of the 'uncles' weren't so nice." She pulled up her sleeve and exposed the three-inch scar that ran along her forearm. "Uncle Sebastian liked to play with Swiss knives."

She rolled down the sleeve of her left arm and then pulled the cotton material away from her right shoulder. "Then there was Uncle Wayne who liked to hit me with the buckle of a belt."

"The bastards should have been strung up." The anger in his deep timbre soothed a part of her that she'd hidden for so long.

"There are others but eventually CPS was called enough times for me to be removed from my mother's care. My aunt, who lived in Houston, kind of knew about me but she and my mother had lost contact years ago. Aunt Bea is one of the sweetest people alive. My mom could be, too. But Aunt Bea was the kindest person ever and had the biggest heart. She was here in Houston, doing her own thing. She and my mom didn't grow up together because there was a big age gap. They weren't close," she said.

"Couldn't agree more about your aunt." Kurt's gaze dropped to her forearm and she could've sworn white-hot anger flashed behind his eyes.

"Without her, I never would have degrees hanging on the wall or a job as a college professor. I ended up being bounced around in foster care for a few years until word got to my aunt that I was out there and could use someone to take care of me. She got me when I was twelve. Right before the teenage years, which I'm sure was fun for her. I tried to make them as easy on her as possible. The truth is that I was so afraid she'd realize that she'd made a mistake and would turn me back *in that I pretty much made straight As and washed the dishes every day before she got home from work. Then, one night after dinner when I jumped up to start clearing the table, she asked me to sit back down. She took my hand in hers."* She paused long enough to get a handle on the emotions trying to form as tears in her eyes. *"I remember it so vividly because it was the first time she tried to reach out and touch me…I was probably fourteen and a half years old by then…but it was the first time that I didn't involuntarily flinch. I wanted human contact, which I hadn't had."*

"Of course not. Not after the way you were treated. I'm surprised you were able to trust anyone after that," he said.

"Looking back, I think Aunt Bea found me at just the right time. If that had gone on much longer, I think I was starting to hit a breaking point. It may have been what motivated my caseworker to see if there was someone out there who she could find to take me. Overall, I was a good kid who needed to catch a break," she admitted. *"Aunt Bea didn't have to do it, but she saved my life. No question in my mind about it. So, when she needs me, the question isn't if I should jump, it's how high does she need me to go."*

He sat there in silence for a long moment. It wasn't awkward, like she half expected it to be after spilling so many personal secrets, but it was a comfortable silence. Like a moment of quiet instead of prayer when people just sit in each other's presence and are still.

9

Kurt let Arianna's words sink in. There was so much about her that surprised him. Her past. How she'd overcome it. She was well spoken and had worked for everything she'd gotten. He'd almost gotten mixed up with the wrong crowd before dating Stacy.

His mother had been pretty quick to shut it down and he was grateful to this day that he listened. She'd given him the statistics about kids who get on a wrong path and what that ended up doing to their lives.

In Arianna's case, life had come at her pretty hard, early on. She was able to turn that into something besides anger and frustration, like so many people did when life handed them heartache after heartache.

"It's amazing that you've turned out to be a kind and compassionate person. You are amazing." The words came out low, but he hoped she picked up on how much he meant them. He had so much respect for her after hearing about her upbringing. "Thank you for telling me about your past. It means a lot to me that you would trust me."

She sat there for a long moment, too. He figured she needed a minute.

"I hope you know how incredible you are. Most people don't survive that let alone get to the other side and become successful."

"Thank you, Kurt." Her voice was low and it sent sparks flying inside his chest. It was the freakin' Fourth of July in there. "You have *a great kid in there. I'm sure trying to do this on your own even with my aunt's help has to be scary at times."*

"It has its moments." He smiled.

"You're doing all the right things. You're doing an amazing job with her and that's why she's who she is. Paisley is lucky to have someone so devoted to her that he would literally put his life on the line to save hers." There was a wistful quality to her voice, and he could understand why, given her background, and was even more impressed with the things she'd accomplished. Being abused and then bounced around in the system didn't usually produce college professors. Her background didn't usually lead to the kind of life she had now, well-rounded, kind, giving. Loyalty.

"You already said you're a college professor. How is it that you can step in and help with Paisley?" he asked. She'd put her entire life on hold the second her aunt had called and was still there so that her aunt would rest easier. There was the attraction that Kurt felt, that insta-attraction, the physical kind, but getting to know her and being able to see the real her was like a jackhammer on the cement around his heart.

And in so many ways, he felt like he could really breathe. He told himself that he would like to have a friend like her, that he would like to have a role model like her in Paisley's life. But there was so much more to it than that.

"I'm on sabbatical from teaching this term. I needed a break to get out of the States and do more fieldwork."

"When do you leave?" he asked, cursing the timing. He finally met someone he'd like to get to know better and she was about to take off.

She laughed and glanced at the clock. "I was supposed to be on a flight two hours ago. An overnighter to Peru. I was going there to study indigenous people and the way they communicate in a modern world."

"What about another flight?" He didn't want her to miss out and suddenly felt selfish for tying up her day. He'd been so focused on protecting Paisley that he hadn't even asked what else Arianna might have on her plate.

"It's fine. It's just a side project. I just needed to regroup and get away for a while. I can pick up on the trip once my aunt is settled and feeling better."

"She's lucky to have you." And so was he. That kind of devotion and loyalty was a little too rare in the modern world. It was a rare find in a person. He wanted her to know how special he thought that quality was in a person.

"I hope so," she said.

Paisley stirred in the next room. Kurt was to his feet in two seconds. In another few, he was at the crib. He realized that Arianna was right beside him.

His angel rolled around a couple of times before finding a good position and then falling back into a deep sleep. Arianna took his hand—and firebolts shot through him at the intimacy—before leading him back into her aunt's bedroom.

She let go and reclaimed her seat.

"I've gotten a few texts from my aunt today. I figured you should know so we could come up with a plan. She's pretty determined to come here from the hospital tomorrow. She believes she's going to be released around noon."

"That's fast," he said before quickly adding, "That's good news."

"You know how she can be once she gets something in her head. It can be hard to talk her down." She laughed, breaking some of the tension. "But I'm guessing you've had plenty of experience with that by now."

Well, he really laughed now. Bea Calaway was stubborn in the most sincerely honest way. When she dug her heels in, she meant it and it was usually for the better. Like when she used to force him to *get a couple hours of sleep in those early weeks after losing Stacy. He would just want to be by Paisley's side twenty-four-seven.* "Yep, I've seen that side to her. She forced me to sit down, to go downstairs and let my daughter sleep. She eventually convinced me that I didn't need to be by her side all hours of the day. That she would continue to breathe and would be okay. And if she woke up and cried that Bea would get to her. That I didn't have to be right here next to her, crashed on the floor. So, yeah, I know how stubborn she can be." *Man, he'd been lost in those early days.*

"When she knows what's best, she won't take no for an answer."

"That is the gospel truth. Well, you know your aunt better than I do. What do you think?"

"To come here, she wants to get a car service using her cell phone. Just order one." *Arianna issued an exacerbated-sounding sigh.*

"First of all, there's no way she's leaving the hospital in a random car," he countered. "I'll pick her up."

"I can help."

"Secondly, she lives here most of the time, so I've got no problem with her coming back here unless you think it's a bad idea," he said.

"I can postpone my trip. I have the time off from the university. There's nothing really stopping me from hanging around until she's well enough to step into her job. I'm not sure if that's something—"

"You'd be willing to do that?"

"Of course. Like I said, she's all the family I have. I'd move heaven and earth for her. She deserves someone willing to drop everything to help her because that's what she does. It's the least I can do for her after everything she's done for me."

"I would personally love for you to stay here." *He was probably a little too enthusiastic with the way he said that. He was tired and wasn't exactly one to pull any punches. Speaking his mind, behind honest, had gotten him pretty far in life so far. And it was true. He did want her to stick around for reasons that soothed his heart and were probably dangerous.*

"Good. I want to stay and help. Thank you for spending this time with me to let me get to know you better. I feel a little like I know you through my aunt. She has only nice things to say about you. And, of course, I know you through Paisley. The two of you don't look a lot alike until you smile. She has your smile. And she's smart and funny. I feel like knowing her personality and now that I've talked to you, I see the resemblance. She is an easy baby and she smiles a lot but when she's learning something new, you can see the wheels turning. She can be a little intense and I'm seeing that she gets that from her dad."

"I'll take all the compliments I can get and all the credit that anyone's willing to give me because, down deep, I truly think that kid is turning out well despite me."

Talking to someone, connecting, those things had been missing far too long in Kurt's life. Even before with Stacy. To be honest, he'd thought when she'd told him that she was pregnant before their timeline that maybe she'd gotten pregnant on purpose because she was lonely and maybe he'd been so focused on work that he'd neglected her in a lot of ways in their relationship.

Let her down?

He thought they had time. Time to hit the reset button on their relationship. Time to get themselves on good footing again. Just time.

As it turned out, life had its own sense of timing.

There was a moment happening between him and Arianna. Something in the air shifted and he became aware of the fact that he was in the same room, a couple of feet, from an incredibly intelligent and beautiful woman. One who had a sense of humor and was easy to talk to. He couldn't remember the last time he just talked to someone. Not forced or polite conversation but really talked to someone about what was on his mind and troubling him. Learning about what she'd been through, as much as he hated hearing it, caused him to respect her even more after what she was able to accomplish in life despite the odds against her.

What she was able to overcome…those people were rare in life. He'd learned that the hard way.

"We should probably try to get some shut-eye. That little princess in the next room is an early riser." He didn't want to leave the room. He didn't want to stop talking to Arianna. He didn't want to end this night. But tomorrow would hit hard and fast. Without sleep, he wouldn't exactly be bringing his A-game.

Too many nights he'd dozed on the couch, not wanting to go to bed. They'd bought this house and tried to move in before the birth. Paisley came a week early and he closed on the house the morning she was born.

Little did he know that night would change his life in so many great ways and, also, deal him the toughest blow he figured he'd ever face.

"Goodnight, Kurt." Man, her voice had a way of traveling all over him, reaching deep in his chest.

"Goodnight." Kurt checked on Paisley one more time before stepping over the gate.

The guest room in this house was upstairs and the master was down the hall from the office. Often times, he would sleep in the guest room to be closer to Paisley.

Tonight, he needed to put an entire floor between him and Arianna because she was awakening parts of him that had been shut down. She made him want to reach out and touch her, to press his lips against hers.

Under the circumstances, not a good idea. The last thing he needed was to complicate his relationship with his babysitter by making a move on her niece.

Despite Arianna giving him signs, he didn't think it was a good idea to do any of the things he wanted, like claim those gorgeous pink *lips of hers. She was temptation on a stick and having her under the same roof kept his blood pressure racing. More of that concrete casing cracked as he'd gotten to know her better.*

It had been a really long time since he'd been on a first date. He chuckled as he took the stairs two at a clip. His game was definitely not strong. He was ready to ask out his babysitter's niece.

Good one, Johnson. Despite having that last name his entire life, he questioned it. Hell, he questioned his whole identity now. It was impossible not to wonder what his birth father was like. What his habits were. Hobbies.

Getting ready for bed didn't take long. He doubted he would be able to sleep in anything more than fifteen-minute bursts. It was amazing how well he could function on very little sleep. Plus, he wanted to think more about who might want to kidnap his daughter and what the person would have to gain. There had to be a motive. An opportunist seeking ransom. A newly discovered brother seeking revenge. An uncle trying to stir up the pot or detract attention away from himself. A judge wanting leverage to force Kurt into dropping the investigation into a container filled with humans.

All those thoughts rolled around in his head. And yet, his reasoning for ending the conversation with Arianna had more to do with the connection he felt with her—a connection so strong that it caused him to question everything he thought he knew about love.

10

Arianna dozed off thinking about Kurt Johnson. What she felt toward him in such a short time was a puzzle she doubted she'd solve anytime soon but couldn't stop turning over in her mind. There was something about getting to know someone under fire—something that stripped a person down to the core of who they really were without all the fluff. She might not know his favorite color or sport's team, but she knew intimate details about him and his life.

Cuzya let off rapid-fire barks, interrupting her thoughts. A piercing noise split the air. Paisley wailed in the next room. Arianna threw off the covers and hopped out of bed. She darted into the next room before she realized there was a weird smell in the house.

And something that set her lungs on fire. Smoke?

Coughing, she got to Paisley at the same time as Kurt. A haze in the room made it difficult to see clearly.

"What's going on?" she managed to ask as she started coughing. The burning sensation in her nose confirmed her fear. Fire.

Panic gripped her as she locked gazes with Kurt. The house was going up in flames in shocking speed. Paisley coughed as Kurt covered her mouth and nose with a blanket. Cuzya stood barking toward the hallway.

"Follow me," Kurt said as he hugged his daughter to his chest and ran into the adjoining room. He immediately handed his daughter over as heat from the hallway bore down on them. Smoke thickened and she was shocked at how fast the house seemed to become engulfed.

The two-story craftsman had a covered front porch. He climbed halfway out and called for Cuzya. She followed. Then, he took Paisley from Arianna before helping her out.

This probably was the time to mention her fear of heights as she gripped onto his arm and squeezed her eyes shut. "I don't. Can't."

"Just breathe." Those two words poured over her in that low timbre of his.

She reminded herself to slow down as she felt her chest squeeze like suddenly her shirt was four sizes too small.

Breathe.

"Do you trust me?" Kurt's voice broke through the rising panic inside her.

"Yes." She risked a glance at him. There was something about his face, the honesty, the confidence that helped her take the next step toward the edge.

"We're going to sit down now," he said. "We're going to be fine, but we have to hurry."

Kurt sat down, keeping eye contact with Arianna as she followed suit.

"Sorry. I've always been afraid of heights since I was a little girl."

"Don't be sorry. We'll work around it best as we can. As long as you trust me, we'll all get down."

Cuzya was circling and barking. She'd roused the neighborhood dogs, who joined in her chorus.

"Hold on there. I'm coming." Raul must've seen the blaze and heard the barking noise. After what happened yesterday morning, he was most likely watching the house anyway. He ran toward the house from next door with a ladder in his hands.

Arianna could see the flames inside the house and smoke started bellowing out the windows.

Kurt took her hand and scooted the three of them toward the ladder. The porch covering was high off the ground and she didn't risk a glance over the side.

"You're doing great," he said. "Keep looking at me and Paisley."

Paisley was quietly crying against her father's chest. Arianna reached out to stroke the little girl's hair. Focusing on Paisley was better than thinking about what would come next and, in fact, kept her heart rate from spiking again from anxiety.

Raul yelled up. "Ladder's secure."

Kurt caught her gaze and held it. Paisley leaned toward Arianna, so she took the little girl from her father's arms.

"Will you be all right up here if I hand Cuzya off?" Kurt asked, looking a little stunned at the move.

She nodded, hoping it was true. "Yes, go." The faster he went, the sooner he could come back for Paisley.

Kurt picked up the dog with one strong arm and then navigated the ladder. He returned a few seconds later for Paisley. Arianna scooted as close to the edge as she could get. Normally, she'd squeeze her eyes shut but instead focused on Paisley. "It's okay, sweet girl. Your daddy has you now."

Kurt took his daughter as Arianna tried to scoot a little closer.

As he disappeared down the ladder, her heart battered her rib cage.

"Roll onto your stomach," he shouted.

Breathe.

She did. The roof had a slight slope and she realized Cuzya must be very agile to have run circles up here. Facing the building, she watched as flames licked the window. It was only a matter of time before this place collapsed.

It dawned on her that her purse, wallet and phone were inside. There was no going for them now. They were lost at this point.

"Ease backward and keep your eyes on the house." Kurt's voice was a study in calm.

She felt his hands on her calves as she moved toward him. And then the backs of her thighs. He guided her until her feet were secured on a ladder rung. With his body behind her, she gripped the ladder and took it one step at a time.

A siren wailed in the distance as she reminded herself to breathe and keep going until her feet reached the ground. And her feet were bare because her shoes were neatly tucked underneath the bed.

"Let's step back." Kurt urged Arianna across the street as he did his best to calm Paisley. Raul had Cuzya secured with him.

Flames engulfed the home in surprising speed.

"Is everybody okay?" Raul asked. His chest heaved and he must've taken in some of the smoke while he was helping because he had a coughing fit.

They were safe. They made it out. They were going to be fine.

Arianna tried to catch her breath as she called Cuzya over. She dropped down on one knee and hugged the Rhodesian ridgeback as the first tears fell.

Based on Paisley's screams, her lungs were in good working order. She was sucking in bursts of air and Kurt was doing his best to calm her. Since, sometimes, the best medicine was a distraction, Arianna stood up and made bunny ears. She started hopping around and singing Paisley's favorite bunny song.

"Scooping up the field mice," she sang softly as the fire raged across the street.

The little girl's screams slowed, and she giggled through a few tears when Arianna sang, "And bopped them on the head."

Paisley giggled out loud as she stuffed her fingers in her mouth. Those red-rimmed eyes were heartbreaking, but Arianna got a lot of satisfaction in being able to divert her attention and make her smile.

Kurt's jaw nearly hit the ground when Paisley leaned toward Arianna and threw her hands out, wanting to be held. She immediately locked gazes with Kurt to make sure it was okay with him.

Eyes wide, he gave an almost imperceptible nod.

"Come here, sweet girl." Arianna held his daughter, quietly finishing the song.

Normally, an event like this would send Arianna's stress levels through the roof but there was something comforting about being with Kurt and his kid. Focusing on getting Paisley's spirits up had brought up hers. Breathing had become automatic again and the pressure in her chest had lightened up considerably.

Anxiety was a peculiar beast. One that she usually overcame by slowing down, reminding herself to breathe and telling herself the state of her body was a temporary overreaction that felt very real.

The brain was a powerful tool. That also meant when it tricked her, it went all-in.

A firetruck roared around the corner, too late to salvage much of the house's contents. Getting on a flight in the near future just went up in flames along with so many other things. No ID equaled no travel. The thought of no cell phone gave her anxiety, so she pushed that out of her mind. She would need to be practical and rebuild the contents of her purse, like credit cards, debit card, driver's license.

That could wait a few hours. There wasn't much she could do about it right now anyway. Her car was parked in front of the neighbor's house because there'd been a squad car directly in front of Kurt's. She had an extra set of keys in her apartment but no door key to her unit. The office would have one, though.

Keeping only one credit card in her wallet and one at home for emergencies seemed like the smartest decision she'd made in a while. Her laptop was at home, too. At least she wouldn't have to worry about replacing it.

Kurt's insurance would probably cover any valuables, but she'd left all those at home. She'd planned to run home to get a change of

87

clothes before they picked up her aunt. After nine a.m., she could get a key from the office and fill a few of the voids. She had a spare purse and kept her old licenses in a metal file box at home. She could start from there.

It took singing through the bunny song again and talking about the fire truck in great detail before the blaze was finally put out. Kurt was busy with a fireman and a cop, giving a statement. Cuzya stayed at Arianna's side. The dog's devotion to Paisley would make anyone a pet lover.

The occasional glance from Kurt kept a very different blaze alive in her. The minute their gazes locked warmth spread through her. Those little campfires were lit again and despite the circumstances, she felt like everything would work out.

Kurt's truck had been spared the fire. As she mentally ran through the contents of her purse, a firefighter emerged with the singed bag in hand.

"Mr. Johnson asked me to bring this to you," the man said. He was covered in sweat and had on full gear with his visor up. He held out her half-ravaged bag. "It's safe to touch. There's water damage, though."

Part of the strap had literally burned away.

"Thank you." She took the offering and realized much of the to-do list she'd been creating in her head wouldn't need to happen. There was more relief as she pulled the bag closer and looked inside. Yep, she had a wallet and keys. Thank heaven for small miracles.

An EMT followed the firefighter. He checked their pulse ox, listened to their lungs and then cleared them with the recommendation they stop by their doctor's office or ER if they experienced chest pain.

Kurt stood with Raul, a fireman, and a cop for a few more minutes as Arianna took a seat on the curb next to Cuzya. Paisley stood on her own, holding onto Arianna's hands to keep balance. And the looks she got from Kurt melted more of her resolves.

So much so, she had to remind herself how badly her last relationship with a single father had been. Because the way Kurt looked at her now made her want to forget the betrayal and broken heart and logic that warned it would be a huge mistake.

She hadn't loved her ex the way her heart said she could love Kurt. Forget all the arguments against insta-love or romantic love. She'd never believed in love at first sight. But after talking to Kurt long into the night, she realized there was something very different about this man. Something special and lasting. And she knew him on a soul level.

KURT FINISHED GIVING his statement and thanked the firemen, officer, and his neighbor. Between Cuzya's early barking and Raul's quick thinking, Paisley and Arianna were spared. Kurt was alive.

His hands fisted at his sides thinking that anything could have happened to either of them along with the pet who'd been at his side for the past eight years. Cuzya had that loyalty gene down pat and she'd extended it to Paisley the day she came home from the hospital.

Thinking about who could've done this and why sent a firebolt of anger rocketing through Kurt. Thinking about the damage that could've been done to the people under his roof. Thinking about the fact someone had come for his family not once, but twice caused every muscle in his body to tense. He was wired so tight he thought a muscle might snap.

Getting to the bottom of this was his only priority from here on out.

His vehicle seemed fine to drive. Most things were replaceable. No big deal. Except a few items that were from Stacy and could never be substituted. She'd gone to crochet classes so she could make a blanket for Paisley's crib, which she'd done.

Firemen couldn't save it. In fact, they said Paisley's entire room came through the living room ceiling. Nothing could likely be salvaged. Not her crib. Not her favorite stuffed bunny. Not her special blanket.

The last picture he'd taken of Stacy, the one of her cradling her baby bump days before giving birth, was most likely gone or severely damaged. He didn't take for granted the fact the people in the house were safe and had survived. But he couldn't ignore the losses.

11

"I'm sorry about your home." Arianna's calm voice cut through Kurt's emotions as he let those words sink in. Even though he'd lived there for a short twelve months, the place felt like home. This is the place he'd brought his daughter home from the hospital and the place he'd become a family.

Seeing more than half of it burned to ashes...

It also reminded him that the bastard who had tried to kidnap his daughter had upped the ante. Rather than go down the road that built up unproductive anger—anger that couldn't go anywhere—he leaned into Arianna and pressed a kiss to those soft pink lips of hers. The second their lips made contact, a bomb detonated inside Kurt. He was almost knocked back a step. Digging his heels in, he deepened the kiss as her lips moved against his. He pulled back and the glittery look in her eyes stirred his heart. Then, there was her smile. She raked her top teeth over her bottom lip, leaving a silky trail. One he couldn't afford to stare at much longer for fear he'd close the gap between them a second time.

The moment happened between them too quickly, but the impact would be long lasting.

And that was as far as anything between them could go at the moment because he had an unknown enemy to stop before he erased everything dear to Kurt. His mind was spinning, trying to think of who he'd upset this much. An enemy was bad. An unknown enemy was downright lethal.

"There isn't much left, and it won't be safe to go inside for a while. Not to mention the fact it's considered a crime scene now," he said as Paisley babbled and blew spit bubbles.

Kids were so resilient. She was happy as a lark standing there, holding onto Arianna's hands, blissfully unaware she'd lost everything. As grounded as he believed himself to be, there'd be no shaking off the losses easily.

"My apartment is small, but it would do as a place to hang out until we find bigger accommodations," she offered. "I don't have any kids stuff there but I'm sure we could make a couch work for her nap."

"We could do that." He glanced around as the first responders taped off his property, marking it as a crime scene. A thought occurred to him. This person meant business. "On second thought, I don't want to bring this jerk to your doorstep. Whoever did this seems to be fixated on getting to me or her. That's putting you in danger."

Arianna was shaking her head. "I think I know where you're going with this and I want to be here for the both of you."

"What if it's too risky?"

"I'm a grown woman, capable of deciding what I'm willing or unwilling to do," she countered, all the desire he'd seen a moment ago turned into defiance.

"True. I wouldn't want it any other way. As your aunt's employer, I'm responsible for her. Since you're stepping in for her, I can't help but feel responsible for you, too."

She didn't immediately respond and that gave him hope. Was she seriously considering what he was saying? This was bigger than standing up to a bully. This could cost her life. As much as he wanted her, no, needed her, risking her safety was too high a price to pay.

He also acknowledged that he was between a rock and a hard place considering he had Paisley to think about. His daughter needed someone who could care for her. Kurt was perfectly capable of taking care of his own daughter. The problem was that it would be next to impossible to keep some semblance of a schedule with Paisley and track down a dangerous criminal.

"I'm here. I'm staying." Her loyalty meant everything to him, but he couldn't stand back while she put her life on the line for him.

Unless…

Levi's offer to stay at the ranch crossed his mind. Security at the ranch would be much stronger than anything he could drum up in a few hours. Then, there was the obvious fact that he no longer had a home to go to. He couldn't be completely certain that a McGannon wasn't involved. Like he'd told Levi, he'd know if he looked in the eyes of someone who tried to kidnap his daughter. The situation had escalated now, and he was looking for someone capable of murder.

"I need to make a call," he said to Arianna, fishing his cell out of the pocket of his jeans where he also found the key to his truck. It was a good thing he hadn't undressed because that meant he still had a phone and the key to his truck, which had the car seat in it. Small miracles. He'd take it.

Arianna cocked her head to one side and her eyebrows drew together.

He tapped on Levi's name and said, "How ready are you to meet my family?"

Her eyes widened in response and before she could respond, Levi's voice came on the line.

"What's wrong?" Levi's question threw Kurt for a loop. Before he could respond, Levi continued, "You don't seem like the type who would be calling unless the roof was caving in."

"You're not too far off." The comment would've been funny if it wasn't so true and Kurt wasn't staring at the evidence. "Someone set my house on fire."

Levi bit out a few choice words that Kurt wouldn't repeat in front of his daughter. "Is everyone okay?"

"Shaken up, but we're all fine."

"We have a guest house on the property that you're welcome to stay in. There's plenty of room in the main house, too. I'd just be more comfortable if Uncle Donny slept under a different roof than you guys until we get to the bottom of this," Levi admitted.

Again, having a brother ready to jump in on Kurt's behalf was as strange as a dog with four eyes.

"Is my dog going to be a problem? I don't go anywhere without her," he stated.

"On this ranch? There's plenty of room to roam. And most of our dogs come in and out of the house when they please. We have a couple that prefer the barn. It's safe to say that animals rule on the McGannon property," Levi said without hesitation.

It was still too early to make a ruling, but he liked what he saw so far from the McGannons. Extra eyes on his family would be a welcomed sight.

"Is the guest house large enough to accommodate my babysitter and her niece?" he asked.

"Four of you and a dog won't be an issue," Levi said with confidence. "What time can I tell security you'll be arriving?"

Kurt took in a sharp breath. "I need to tie up some business before heading that way."

"When you say business…what do you mean exactly?" There was a protectiveness to Levi's tone that caught Kurt off guard. Getting used to having siblings was going to be a wild ride.

"Not what you're thinking. I have my daughter with me. I literally mean that I need to stop by my office since I won't be going back to any of my usual places until the person behind this is caught." He didn't say locked behind bars because at this point all he could think about was ripping the guy responsible apart, limb by limb if he had to.

Mess with him and he wouldn't back down. Mess with his child and he'd come hunting.

"I'll let the others know that you're coming. Everyone except Uncle Donny. I don't want to tip him off," Levi thought along the same lines as Kurt on that front.

"Anyone else I need to be worried about?"

"I'm probably being too hard on Uncle Donny. We've never seen eye-to-eye. I don't let my guard down around him and..." Levi stopped. There was an emotion present in his tone that Kurt couldn't readily identify. It took a second to realize what it was. Guilt.

Working on the ranch alongside his father, did Levi blame himself for not being in the equipment room when his father took a spill that landed him in the hospital?

Considering Levi's personality, the way he seemed to take personal responsibility for everyone around him, the guy would be hard on himself if he thought something slipped past. Kurt wondered if Levi was like their father.

"I look forward to getting to know the others. Right now, I'd like to stay low," he said.

"We're on the same page. I'll tell a few people. The ones who need to know," Levi promised. He seemed like a man of his word.

Kurt thanked him and Levi promised to text over the address to the ranch after they ended the call. The text came almost immediately. Levi seemed to be reliable and trustworthy. Those were big steps to take with anyone, especially someone who had no real reason to care about Kurt and every reason to resent him.

"READY?"

Arianna figured that was a loaded question. She picked up Paisley and nodded. "She'll need to eat soon. She's fully awake now."

"No chance she'll go back to sleep in the truck," Kurt agreed.

"No sleep," Paisley parroted and that made both Kurt and Arianna laugh. It was a rare bright spot in an otherwise dark morning.

"We can stop by the store on the way into my office," he said.

"Actually, I need to swing by my house first. Could we pick up supplies and feed her at my apartment?" She pointed toward her bare feet.

"Good idea." He had on jeans and a T-shirt, the same outfit from last night, and also would need a pair of shoes.

She looked down at his feet and he must've read her thoughts at that point because he said, "I always keep a pair of running shoes in the gym bag in my truck. I used to go to the gym regularly before this one was born."

Arianna handed over the kiddo and walked with him to his truck. She climbed in the passenger side while he buckled his daughter in her car seat in the back. Arianna searched the contents of her purse. The bag was in bad shape and everything inside was soggy. With two fingers, she removed her soaked wallet. Water dripped onto her lap after she buckled in.

Her plastic-covered ID survived as did her credit card. This would make life easier. Digging past a soggy gum packet, she located her cell. "Remind me to pick up a replacement charger at the store."

She highly doubted the one in her purse had survived.

"Gotcha." Kurt claimed the driver's seat.

Risking a glance over at him, her pulse ratcheted up a few notches. Her eyes dropped to his lips and a fiery heat ripped through her. Thoughts of the kiss they'd shared ravaged her thoughts. It was probably sad the kiss was the first time she'd practically melted in someone's arms. Or felt so thoroughly kissed. She could only imagine what going further with a man like Kurt would be like—most definitely the best sex of her life if the kiss could be trusted. And then what? Much like a raging wildfire, she'd be devastated when he was gone. And he would be gone. She couldn't allow that kind of hurt into her life.

Could she?

KURT FILLED up the tank while he was at the convenience store, all the while checking their surroundings for anyone or anything that looked suspicious. He'd already put on his running shoes before they left home and he missed his boots already.

His favorite boots were among the many possessions he'd lost. Reminding himself that boots can be replaced, he rounded up his purchases, paid, and then headed back to the truck.

He also figured that he might as well fill Arianna in on what Devin had said yesterday about the judge. It dawned on him that he hadn't canceled the alarm company representative who was supposed to show in an hour.

Kurt made the call to cancel the appointment, reassuring Suzy the bonuses were still good. He explained the house fire and told her that he'd be in touch when he had a new residence.

"My aunt is going to be worried sick," Arianna finally said after he ended the call. "I've been pre-occupied with everything going on and didn't think about how we're going to tell her what's happened."

"I'm planning to bring her with us to the McGannon ranch," he said. "You heard that earlier, right?"

"It's a good idea," she agreed. "Sounds like the safest possible place to be while law enforcement figures out who could be trying to hurt you. Plus, Aunt Bea will love the ranch. She's big on animals as you probably already know, and always said she'd have a zoo if she could. Working for other people and basically living in someone else's house makes it difficult for her to keep her own pet but I can tell you that she pretty much claimed Cuzya as hers from the minute they met."

"Cuzya feels the same." His loyal companion was currently curled up in the back seat next to the car seat. He constantly checked his mirror to ensure they weren't being followed as he navigated the roads to her apartment. Despite the morning's circumstances, Kurt was at ease being with Arianna.

Thankfully, she lived in a building with gated parking. He pulled in and she instructed him to park in her spot. The garage was meant for smaller cars, but he navigated into the tight space.

He climbed out of the driver's side and retrieved Paisley, who was chatting away. Man, to be that innocent again. That was part of the magic of having her. Getting to see the world through pure eyes and a pure heart. She reminded him of everything good about being alive.

"I can grab the grocery bag," Arianna offered.

The way she pitched in and the scene of the three of them together gave him the first glimpse of what it would be like to remarry. Hearing the word in his head made him snap into betrayal mode. But was it?

Guilt hit him just as hard. But would Stacy want him to live the rest of his life alone? Would she want Paisley to have a mother figure? No one could replace her actual mother. There was no question in his mind there. It would be like having another kid to replace Paisley, an awful and misguided sentiment.

This was the exact kind of thing he wished he could get Stacy's opinion on. She had no family to speak of once her mother moved overseas. No sister or mother—at least not one who knew her—that he could ask in his wife's absence.

Face it. He wanted absolution for the guilt he carried with him. Guilt that made him think he had to be punished for the rest of his life for letting Stacy down. Guilt because she was gone and he was still alive. Guilt that made him question every day of their last year together. Had he treated her right? Did she know how much he loved her? Was she aware that he would've traded his life for hers?

At some point in the blur of the past year, a doctor handed him information on survivor's guilt. He'd tucked it inside the drawer of his desk, figuring the guy had it wrong. One of the many late nights when Kurt lay staring at the ceiling, unable to sleep, he retrieved the brochure and read enough to realize the doc was probably right.

Kurt wasn't done punishing himself, but he did hang onto the material. Was it time to think about having a future again?

He followed Arianna to the elevator and then to her apartment on the seventh floor. The best way to describe her apartment was cozy modern. The sofa was light colored and had coordinating chairs nestled around a fireplace. The place was neat and orderly. She had a spot for everything. Everything. There were plenty of sharp edges on the coffee table and not a speck of dirt to be found.

The balcony would give him nightmares if he lived there with Paisley. Definitely not a kid-friendly environment. What had he expected?

And why was he disappointed?

12

"**K**itchen's around here."

Kurt noticed there were only bar height chairs pushed up to an island in the open-concept kitchen. There wasn't anything wrong with the place. In fact, it was clean and tastefully decorated. So, what was missing?

The answer came to him almost immediately, the warmth in her personality.

Cuzya walked around like she was looking for a place to sleep. She curled up in front of the fireplace and dozed off. The morning must've taken a lot of energy out of her.

"Make yourself at home." She turned around and must've seen a look on his face. "Everything okay?"

"Yes." He jumped into action, joining her in the kitchen. "Everything is so…perfect and clean. I'm afraid to set her down."

"Oh, right. Sorry about that. It's a sublet and the furniture came with. It's not exactly my taste but I've been too busy to worry about getting my stuff out of storage. I'm rarely home anyway and, even though this isn't my aesthetic, it's pretty enough. My ex-boyfriend never liked coming here with his…" she let the sentence die.

The shot to Kurt's heart was not only unjustified but caught him off guard. The two of them weren't in a relationship and he had no right to feel the possessiveness that he did despite the kiss they'd shared that he couldn't shake out of his thoughts.

The draw to Arianna wasn't something he was accustomed to, which put his mind at war with his heart.

Figuring it wasn't his place to ask, he redirected the conversation. "All I need is an unbreakable bowl or plate, and something to clean out her sippy cup so I can pour some milk in.

"Mmmm." Paisley always did that when she heard her favorite drink mentioned.

"That's right," he said with a smile, trying to shake off the tension of the past twenty-four hours—tension that would have been a lot worse without Arianna by his side.

How hard was he falling for the woman that the mere mention of her ex-boyfriend got him riled up? Were his feelings too hard, too fast?

The kiss wasn't much more than a peck and yet he'd never felt so much electricity, so much heat or so much promise. His logical side argued it was impossible to really fall in love with someone he didn't know two days ago. His heart argued that he did know her on a deep level. The rest was just details—details he could see himself spending the rest of his life discovering about her.

So, yeah, he had a real good handle on his emotions.

Right now, he needed to refocus. Paisley would get cranky soon if she didn't get her milk. She was already squirming in his arms. She also needed a diaper change. It was a good thing he always kept a bag in his truck.

"Is there a good place to change her?" he asked.

"Bedroom is through there. Would that work?" She pointed toward a hallway by the front door.

"Definitely." He grabbed a diaper on the way in and made do with what little supplies he had to work with, cleaning his daughter with a washcloth. He was pretty proud of his handiwork now, but those early days had been a mess. Don't even get him started on how many times he'd accidently pulled the tape completely off.

He'd learned a lot in a year's time. His babysitter and life experience were both great teachers.

Folding up the soiled diaper, he picked up Paisley and brought both back into the living room. Arianna had set up a spot for him to sit on the sofa and feed Paisley dry cereal. She immediately stretched out her hands toward the sippy cup after locking onto it.

"Mmmmmm."

"Here you go." Arianna seemed to catch onto the importance of the moment, handing over the cup before the excitement turned to frustration and tears. Kids' emotions could be all over the map in the space of ten minutes. All that growing took a toll on even the sweetest babies. "I'll leave you two to it while I grab a quick shower and a change of clothes. Do I have time?"

"Take whatever time you need." He needed to get to the office at some point after it opened. If he was being honest, he'd admit that he wanted to get Paisley and Arianna to the ranch as soon as possible after the fire this morning.

His cell rang after she left the room. He checked the screen to see who was calling and realized he also had a text from Raul. He checked it before answering. Ms. Calaway was doing fine this morning and would be released on schedule. Good news all the way around. Raul was quickly becoming another lifeline.

"Hey, Levi," Kurt answered the call.

"I thought you'd want to know that I have the guest house set up for you. There's a crib in the master and the fridge is stocked. You should have everything you need there. So, what else can I do for you?"

Kurt took a second to shake off the shock. "That's enough. It's more than enough..." Something came to mind, but he wasn't sure how Ms. Calaway would take it. "Actually, my babysitter is due to be released from the hospital around noon. I'd rather not expose Paisley and Arianna to parking lots after we leave my office. I'd prefer to head straight over to the ranch. Any chance you can arrange a pickup for her? She's important to me and—"

"Consider it done. What's her name?" Levi asked.

Kurt gave over the information and thanked Levi again. Having a brother was...nice. Rather than get too caught up in the feeling, he ended the call and focused on feeding his daughter. He was still running the judge scenario in his head. It wasn't good for Kurt's longevity if he angered a dirty judge. He still couldn't figure out how the man would get through the security protocols that had been put in place in his company to vet out dishonest people.

Unless there was some kind of human error involved. It could happen. Things slipped through the cracks. No one was perfect. And then it was also possible that someone was paid to look the other way. Kurt didn't want to consider the possibility that he'd hired a dishonest person. He took pride in his employees.

The police were given access to the files in question. It was only a matter of time before they tracked down the truth. So, the judge was still a possibility.

Again, the trail to him sure was easy. Would a judge be that careless? Or would he feel like he could be because he had people in his pocket? Was he invincible?

Then there was Uncle Donny or one of the other McGannons. Levi trusted his brothers and cousins explicitly and that made Kurt want to believe in them, as well. Could he?

When it came to his daughter's life, he wasn't taking any chances. She was eating the last bite of cereal when Arianna emerged from her bedroom wearing jeans and a blouse. She'd pulled her hair off her face. His gaze moved to those sweet lips of hers where it locked on.

Her tongue darted across her bottom lip, leaving a silky trail.

Kurt blew out a shaky breath and almost laughed. The reaction his body had to her was surprising and he couldn't help but wonder how mind-blowing sex would be if they took things to the next level.

Of course, that would be next to impossible where they were headed. They'd be spending the next couple of days in a guest house on his newly discovered family's ranch with her aunt and his daughter. He couldn't imagine much else that could kill a mood than those circumstances.

Pushing up to standing, he let Paisley sit on the couch and watch the cartoon he'd put on mute, making sure she couldn't roll off and get hurt. Arianna picked up the remote control and turned the volume up enough to create a distraction.

He moved towards her, meeting her halfway, and then properly kissed her. His mouth came down hard on hers and his pulse raced. He brought his hand up to cup her face and better position those sweet lips of hers.

In the background, he heard Paisley's giggles. Those were music to his ears. He'd learned how to tune out repetitive cartoon songs long ago—songs that she loved hearing over and over again. He was used to keeping one ear tuned to her. Cuzya was snoring loudly while curled up but he was used to that sound, as well.

Arianna brought her hands up to his chest and grabbed fistfuls of his shirt. She was intelligent and beautiful, and he was the luckiest guy on earth right now.

He deepened the kiss, driving his tongue inside her mouth and tasting the sweetness.

Pulling apart took some effort but they needed to get on the road and settled at the guest house on the McGannon property, so he could put all his energy into hunting the bastards trying to harm his family.

"We should probably talk about this," he said, referring to the storm they were both caught in.

"You're right. Soon. Not now." The hesitation in her voice warned him that they might be moving too fast for her.

He regrouped and changed the subject, shoving down the tightness in his chest that she could easily walk out of his life when this was over.

"While you were in the shower, I spoke to my..." the word brother came to mind, but it was still too foreign, too unknown, so he went back to, "to Levi. He's arranging for someone to pick up your aunt at the hospital. I'm thinking the less we're on the road or in a spot that someone could be watching the safer it'll be all around."

Her expression took a dive from awareness to concern. She scraped her top teeth across her bottom lip. "That's probably a good idea. Does my aunt know the plan?"

"I haven't contacted her just yet." He glanced at the clock. It was half past eight. "We still have a few hours before noon."

"I can call her and give her the news," she offered. "I've been wanting to check on her this morning anyway."

"Raul sent a text a little while ago. All is well and your aunt will be released as expected," he said, thinking that he needed to respond to Raul's text.

"He's been by her side most of the time?" she asked.

"Mostly. Once he was cleared from the officer to go to the hospital, he's been with her."

She raised an eyebrow and then smiled. "Good for her."

Paisley's show ended and she started blowing raspberries. They both laughed and the break in tension was a nice change of pace.

ARIANNA'S HEART couldn't be any fuller than it was now. So, she seriously needed to rein it in because what was happening between her and Kurt felt a little too real. It shouldn't scare the bejesus out of her. To fall in love with someone should be the most natural thing.

For her, warnings flared. And that was far from normal. Those old tapes started rolling in the back of her mind. The ones that said that the moment she was happy, life would deal a blow.

And this situation couldn't be any more tenuous. Some jerk was literally after Kurt for reasons he and police had yet to figure out, despite having a couple of strong possibilities.

Everyone important to her had left, so why would Kurt be any different? A little voice in the back of her mind pointed out that her Aunt Bea was still there. Even Arianna got one constant.

But going any further with Kurt was like trying to wrangle a forest fire without access to water.

Taking in a deep breath, she said, "I'm still packed from the trip I thought I was going on—"

"Hey, listen, I'm really sorry about that. Are you sure you want to give up Peru? It's not too late to board a flight and I can promise that your aunt will be treated like a queen as she recovers."

Why did those words sting? Why did it feel like he was trying to push her away when, clearly, he was trying to be considerate?

"No. I want to be there for my aunt."

Those last words seemed to hit him just as hard.

"I started tossing clothes out of my suitcase and onto my bed. I don't need that much. I'll just regroup and be back in a minute."

She had no idea how long they'd be staying at the ranch, so it was hard to know how much to bring. She figured a couple days' worth of clothes should do the trick. The ranch had to have a washer and dryer she could use.

He nodded before turning to get his daughter. She cooed happily despite yawning.

Arianna moved into the bedroom and organized the suitcase. She tossed in enough clothes to get her through the next couple of days. Her bag of toiletries was already packed and ready to go, so that was easy. She closed the suitcase, thinking it would be nice to trust another *person for a change. Even at the end of her last relationship, she'd felt burned and embarrassed more than devastated. Corbitt Williams hadn't exactly been the love of her life.*

Had she been playing it safe all these years afraid to risk her heart? The answer to that question was a resounding yes. But habits were hard to break. And as much as she wanted to take a few more steps down that road with Kurt, she couldn't promise herself that she wouldn't pull away at the first sign she might end up hurt.

The counterargument there, and there was always a flipside, was that she never really got to experience love, either.

With danger around every corner, it was easy to table those thoughts for now.

Walking into the living room, suitcase in hand, her heart nearly shredded when she saw how tender Kurt was with his daughter. Sitting on her couch was this big, muscled and sometimes intense man with this sweet innocent little girl who was smiling up at him as he put her hands together for a round of Patty Cake.

Cuzya had moved from in front of the fireplace to next to Kurt's feet but she was out, snoring.

The scene unfolding literally made Arianna's ovaries ache and she was so not that person who sat around and dreamed of having a husband and kids. She'd always seen her life on the perimeter, teaching at university while keeping her mind stimulated. She'd always been more of a live downtown in an apartment type rather than a suburb with a dog person.

And yet, standing there at the doorway, those were exactly the thoughts running through her mind.

Wouldn't it be nice to have a family...well...not exactly any family...this family?

13

Т he drive into work took another half hour from Arianna's house, but Kurt didn't mind. He kept a close eye out for any vehicle that seemed to follow him, grateful none had.

Kurt parked in front of the building, surprised when he didn't see Devin's truck in the lot. It wasn't like his manager not to be at work on time without letting Kurt know. His first thought was that something went wrong with Carla or the baby, but his nerves were on high alert and there was probably a much less stressful explanation. Like Carla had a routine doctor's appointment and Devin forgot to put it on the calendar. This late in the pregnancy would mean weekly appointments.

Or, it was on the calendar and Kurt hadn't checked since he'd been out of pocket this morning and without a laptop.

He did see that Rory was at work and he could stop by his desk and give him an update.

Paisley had fallen asleep on the ride over. He hated waking her. The morning was probably catching up to her and it had been one helluva morning. Cuzya was wide awake.

Kurt glanced around, and it dawned on Kurt that anyone could be watching the office.

Instead of unloading, he texted Rory, asking him to come outside.

Rory was in his mid-thirties and had a young family. He was what most people would describe as short and stocky; in Texas, that meant a height of about five-feet-nine-inches. Rory came up to the window on the driver's side.

"Morning, chief."

Kurt had neglected coming into the office for the past year. He spent most of his time working from home to be near Paisley. Just as he was getting more comfortable with the idea of heading back to the office, all hell seemed to be breaking loose.

The strain on Kurt and Rory's relationship was evidenced in his more formal greeting. They used to be closer. They used to joke around more. They used to have an easy rapport. Rory was a good guy. He'd always been somebody who Kurt felt like he could count on in a pinch.

"Have you seen Devin around this morning?" Had Kurt kidded himself into thinking he could run things from home and still keep his hands in the pie? It sure seemed so.

"Nope. Not sure where he is this morning." Rory shrugged. "Not all that unusual, though."

Devin didn't report to Rory. It was the other way around, but it was surprising that he hadn't updated his second in command to his whereabouts or when he'd be in the office. Even more troubling was the last part about this being typical behavior.

Once Kurt got through this rough patch, and that was the only outcome he could consider, he needed to come back in and tighten up the ship. He'd gotten too lax and the company was neglected. If somebody did really slip past with human trafficking, the writing was on the wall. Not that Kurt blamed Devin. Kurt's company was his responsibility. It was impossible not to feel like he was letting that slip.

"What's going on, chief?" Rory asked. He nodded and smiled at Arianna on the passenger side before his gaze shifted to the backseat and to Paisley.

It was interesting the effect a little girl had on a grown man. The way these big, gruff, ex-football playing guys melted into practical goo around little angels had always made him smile.

It was sweet how all their toughness could melt away in the face of a toothless smile.

"It's been a morning," Kurt decided not to go too far into the details. "An officer will most likely be by to interview Devin and possibly talk to you guys, as well."

Rory straightened up his shoulders. "Everything okay?"

Devin must not have told Rory about the trafficking ring.

"You'll hear about this soon enough because I'm sure it'll be in the news. Someone tried to abduct Paisley from our home and I'm guessing that same person came back this morning and set my house on fire," Kurt said.

The shock on Rory's face said that Devin hadn't prepped him at all.

"That's awful. What can I do?" A muscle in Rory's jaw ticked. He was a family man and had dished all kinds of helpful advice to Kurt during Stacy's pregnancy.

"Cooperate with law enforcement for now. I'm going off the grid for a little while. I'll do my best to keep in touch via cell phone. If you've got any questions or if there's anything here you think I need to be made aware of, I want you to call me on my personal cell."

"You can count on that, chief."

"I appreciate it." On a whim, Kurt decided to ask, "I'm guessing by now you've heard about the container that Devin found."

Rory's eyebrows knitted together in confusion.

"The one used for trafficking?"

"Devin? He didn't find that. I found that." The indignation in Rory's voice made the hairs on the back of Kurt's neck stand. Why would his first in command lie to him and take credit for someone else's work?

"You?"

"Yes, sir. I went to Devin with the find and he told me to let it go and not worry about it. He said we couldn't afford the bad press if word got out. I don't know if it was my place, but I challenged him on that decision. I told him that if word got out it would be ten times worse if we didn't take the lead and go to law enforcement," Rory informed.

Kurt didn't like what he was hearing.

"Has anything else like this happened recently?" he asked.

"No. Just the one, and I was taken back by Devin's response. I meant to talk to you about it when you came in, but..."

He stopped right there like he didn't want to overstep his bounds.

"You were in a tough position. Do you go over your boss's head or stay quiet? For what it's worth, standing up to him was the right thing to do. I apologize for not being around more. Once I get this other investigation behind me, you can believe that's going to change." Kurt had a lot of questions for Devin. His nervous behavior yesterday morning was starting to make a little more sense. He was dishonest about what really happened and that really got to Kurt. His business was built on honesty and trust. This was the exact opposite of those values.

"It'd be nice to see you around more, chief." There was a lot of sincerity in Rory's tone and Kurt definitely needed to make some changes.

He couldn't have someone running his business that he didn't trust, and he needed to have a conversation with Devin about that.

"I appreciate you telling me now," Kurt said. "I will definitely get a handle on this situation. In the meantime, if there's anything else going on up here that doesn't sit well with you, don't hesitate to call me. From here on out, you report directly to me and I'll give the directive, effective immediately. While there's an ongoing investigation, I'm not going to make any other managerial changes. Let's have a sit down when this is over and talk about making a few necessary changes."

"You got it, chief," Rory said. "I look forward to seeing you more."

He glanced at the backseat, at Paisley. "Be careful out there and take care of your family." His gaze shifted from Paisley to Arianna and back to Kurt.

Kurt liked the sound of that. He just wasn't sure if he could go there or if she could, but he couldn't shake the feeling that if he could go there with anybody, it would be with Arianna.

"You, too. Take extra precautions as we work through this. Keep an eye out and make sure you're not being followed. I have no idea how far this situation might extend. Although, I'm certain that Paisley and I have been the targets so far."

Rory was nodding his head.

"All right. You see anything, you hear anything that seems suspect, shoot me a text or give me a call. In the meantime, keep you and your family safe. Take every precaution." A thought occurred to him that Devin wasn't at work because someone had gotten to him. "The same goes for coming into work. If it looks like someone is tailing you, take another lap before heading into the parking lot."

"Okay. I got it."

"All right then, I'll be in touch. And if you see Devin…scratch that. I'll reach out to him myself. It might be better for him if he doesn't know we've had this conversation or that you saw me."

The implications seemed to dawn on Rory. A flash of anger moved behind his eyes. "I hope, for his sake, that he doesn't have anything to do with what's going on."

So did Kurt.

They said their goodbyes before Kurt backed out of the parking spot. Rory stood there in an athletic stance, scanning the street despite the fact very little traffic was on the side road.

Kurt navigated onto the highway, heading west toward the town of Cattle Cove. He'd been on this same highway countless times in his life but only once to take it all the way to this destination. Even then, he hadn't gone to the ranch, but to the hospital instead.

Using Bluetooth technology, Kurt called Officer Forth to update him on the new information he received from Rory.

"The trail to the judge seems to be a dead end. It's possible he was being targeted since he was coming up for re-election. Someone could be trying to sabotage his campaign," the officer said.

"The guy who gave me the information didn't show up for work today," Kurt said.

"I'll swing by his house in a few minutes. I'm not that far from his residence. It won't hurt to do a follow up with him," Officer Forth said.

"I'd appreciate that. There is a possibility out there...and maybe it's just because I don't want to believe one of my own could be involved in anything like this...but he and his family could have been targeted. His wife is pregnant, and I'd sure hate to see her put in jeopardy."

"Duly noted. Either way, it'd be good for me to swing by. First, as a wellness check and then secondly as a follow up just to get a feel," he said.

"Thank you, sir."

"This probably goes without saying, but I have to say it anyway. I know what's happened with your family being under attack can make anyone want to step in. I have to advise you not to intervene with your employee. We can get to the truth faster if he doesn't suspect that you're aware of what's going on. So, I have to ask you not to contact him."

"I understand." Kurt clenched his back teeth so hard he thought they might crack. He did understand. Didn't mean he wouldn't defend his family or not try to find answers.

"Thank you, Mr. Johnson. Trust us. Let us do our jobs on this one and we won't let you down."

Kurt thanked the officer and exchanged goodbyes before ending the call. He rolled his shoulders a couple of times, trying to ease the stress.

"This father of yours. Do you know much about him?" Arianna's voice broke through the silence as Kurt's mind began spinning out on Devin. Kurt appreciated the change in direction.

"No idea. Never met the man. If he's anything like his sons, Levi and A.J., then I'll probably like him. That fact makes me angry because part of me, and that's a large part, wonders how a person who is decent and honorable can ignore one of his children."

"How long has he been in a coma?" she asked.

"More weeks than I want to count. I'm not exactly sure how many," he said. "I do know that there's a lot of uncertainty when someone has been in a coma this long. He has brain wave function and so we do know that he's not brain dead. There's just a lot of uncertainty as to how well he'll do once he wakes up. There have been some recent signs that he might be improving. But, no evidence or proof of a meaningful recovery."

"It's a shame to finally find your birth father and have him taken away before you really have a chance to really get to know the man."

"It's odd. At first, I responded to my uncle reaching out for Paisley's sake. Now, I have to admit that I'm curious about the man. I wonder if, you know, I have any of his personality traits. So, I guess my thoughts have expanded to wanting to know who the man is for me as much as for my daughter."

"Makes a lot of sense to me. How could you not be curious? I never met my father. He was out of the picture long before I had memories. I guess I never really had the urge to find him. If someone reached out to me...when my aunt reached out to me to see if I wanted a home with her, there was no way I wouldn't have gone to meet her. The fact that she turned out to be this amazing person who literally changed my life was the cherry on top."

"The operative word there is wanted."

"What do you mean?" she asked.

"As soon as your aunt found out about you, she came to get you. That's not really what I'm dealing with here. I have an uncle who obviously knew about me. That makes it a different case," he said.

"How? Your uncle knew you existed. Are you one hundred percent certain that your father knew about you?" She paused a beat. "It's possible your mother never told him."

Kurt let that thought settle in for a minute, seeing if it would take seed.

"I always just assumed he knew and turned his back on us. Learning that I have a brother six-months younger than me caused the assumption that my dad had an affair with my mom while he was married to Levi's."

"Your last name is Johnson, right?" she asked.

"Yes," he confirmed.

"Did you ever wonder why your mom didn't give you the last name McGannon? DNA evidence proved it's highly likely Clive McGannon is your father. If she wanted you to know who your father was, wouldn't she have given you his last name? Plus, there's this whole thing about bringing you up on her own. I'm certain that your mother was an amazing woman, so don't take this to mean any disrespect, but she didn't get pregnant alone. It wasn't her fault that she had a baby. Seems like your dad was married to someone else. Maybe your mom never told him about you. Not giving you his last name is a good way to hide paternity."

14

Arianna hoped she wasn't stepping on toes with her assessment. This was just how she saw it and she figured she was coming at it from an objective point of view.

"I never thought of it that way, but it's possible." The wheels seemed to be churning in his mind.

"Have you considered that your mother was trying to protect you all along? It comes out that you're a McGannon in the news and suddenly someone is trying to kidnap your daughter and set your house on fire. The timing can't be ignored regardless of what's going on at work."

"That's true. The work situation is taking on new meaning now that I'm getting more details. It seems like Devin is involved in something that's blowing up in his face."

She nodded.

"I never would've suspected that he would be capable of doing anything wrong. His innocence isn't looking good right now. Evidence is leading me down a path I don't want to go," he admitted. "I do hear you about my family situation, though."

There were two distinct possibilities and hearing that a judge had likely been set up was certainly unsettling. The fact that Kurt's top employee was trying to cover it up and his possible involvement in the situation was bad. Period.

"Along the lines of Devin. You always hear about motive when it comes to crimes. I'm just wondering what he would have to gain by *putting his job in jeopardy and…didn't you say he has a pregnant wife?"*

"The first thing that comes to my mind whenever there's a crime involved is money. He could be strapped for cash. Maybe he's gotten himself in trouble. Something he can't find a way out of. Criminal organizations are strong. They have long tentacles. I haven't been around to lead the ship. It's possible he got in over his head on a situation. I'd like to think that versus him voluntarily working with criminals. Or turning on me and putting my daughter in jeopardy after working for me for the past five years."

"Babies cost a lot of money and need health insurance. Losing his job not only impacts his bank account, but it puts his family at risk. Based on what you've told me about him so far, he doesn't seem like the kind of person who would willingly lose his benefits at a time when he needs them the most," she said. She also understood wanting to see the best in people even when they showed a different hand.

Kurt also had a habit of blaming himself for everything that happened, she'd noticed.

"Do you always do that?" she asked.

He gripped the steering wheel a little tighter. "What?"

"Find a way to blame yourself every time something goes wrong or someone does something that's not your fault?"

He sat there for a long while, seeming to let her questions marinate. She could almost see the gears grinding in his skull.

After taking time to contemplate her words, he said, "Someone points out there's a nose on your face makes it hard to deny there's a nose on your face."

"I didn't mean it in a bad way at all. You take personal responsibility for everyone's safety and that makes you a pretty amazing person in my book. But it also means you're harder on yourself than maybe you should be, and you don't deserve that. That can mess with your head after a while," she pointed out.

117

"Fair point." He paused a couple of beats. "How about this. I will try not to beat up on myself over things other people do that are out of my control."

"Sounds good. Why do I think there's a condition?"

"Because you'd be right." He smiled. "I'll do that if you'll trust me enough to take the first step with me."

"I think that ship has sailed." The kiss back in her apartment made her finally understand how being with someone could make her bones liquid and her legs like rubber.

He chuckled. It was a low rumble in his chest.

"Kurt, if I could take the second step with anyone, it would be you. I'm not going to give you the whole, it's not you because it's me, speech even though it's true. And as much as I want to take another step with you, I don't think it's a good idea. You have Paisley to think about and…" She tried to think of an and. Of another reason it would be a bad idea. Nothing came other than the very obvious fact that she didn't want to risk her heart for fear of it being broken.

"Is it Paisley? Is she the reason?" That sentence was loaded with a whole lot of hurt.

"She's an angel. But I've been involved with a single father before and when that ended, I lost two people. I was heartbroken and I didn't have nearly the feelings for him that I can feel myself developing for you. So, yeah, it's a little bit about Paisley because I'd like to keep her in my life and the best way to do that is to keep an emotional distance from you."

Kurt didn't immediately respond. He kept his eyes on the road ahead as he once again tightened his grip on the steering wheel.

AS KURT TURNED onto the driveway of the McGannon property and was cleared through security, something Levi said was sitting in the back of his mind. It was when he asked Levi if he was offended by the fact that, based on their ages and birthdays, Clive McGannon must've had an affair.

Levi's response?

Relationships were complicated. He knew that his mother and father had loved each other and since she forgave his father, Levi didn't think he had any business not following suit.

Family. Forgiveness. Those had basically been 'F' words most of Kurt's life. The idea of belonging to a big family was appealing in many ways. He knew that there was a lot of track in front of him in getting to know the family. From what he'd seen so far with Levi and A.J., they were good people. If the others were half as decent, Kurt figured they were people he'd want in his life, in Paisley's life.

He wished his mother was around so that he could ask her why she'd kept the big secret. Not once had she discussed his father and he never broached the subject with her, either.

As he drove down the long, tree-lined drive toward the two-story home that had a stone façade and an oversized star of Texas, he saw a massive tree with a tire swing to his left. To his right there was a huge lawn with green grass as far as the eye could see. On that side, a grouping of chairs circled what looked like a firepit.

He glanced at Arianna, whose eyes were as wide as his felt. There was an actual parking lot to the left of the massive home. Beyond that, he noticed as he pulled into a space, there was an impressive set of barns. There was a gravel drive leading to those. Straight in the backyard, it was impossible to miss an actual baseball diamond and before that to the right, a cattle pen.

So, yeah, the money his family had was definitely out of his league and he was doing all right for himself.

"This is where your family lives?" The shock in Arianna's voice mirrored his own.

"I met them at the hospital, so this is my first gander at the place. It's pretty nice. I'm not sure what I expected. Definitely not this." To say the place was overwhelming was a lot like saying youth sports were popular in Texas.

"Are you ready for this?" she asked.

"Is anyone ever ready for this?" Kurt laughed as he cut off the engine and reached for his cell phone. There were several vehicles parked in the lot, everything from trucks to a sedan. The thought of going inside, showing up at the door, felt odd.

Before Kurt could unlock his screen to fire off a text, he caught Levi walking toward him from the main house. "Hold on just a second. Let me see if we're staying here or if there's another plan."

"Okay."

Kurt got out of the truck to meet up with Levi. Kurt extended a hand that Levi looked at and then cocked his head to the side. Rather than take the offering, he pulled Kurt into a bear hug. He was pretty certain every muscle in his body stiffened. And that almost made him laugh, so he relaxed a little bit.

"Good to see you again," Levi said.

"You, too." Kurt was a little stunned by the warm welcome, but it was nice.

"Do you want to follow me to the guest house?" Levi asked.

Kurt nodded.

"We'll go past the cattle pen and make a left before the baseball diamond."

"I have to say. This place is impressive and a little overwhelming," Kurt admitted.

"Growing up here, I'm pretty used to it. The main house is grand. I live on a much smaller place, like most of my brothers and cousins, out on the property. You can get your bearings in the guest house and think about what you might want to build in the future."

Kurt was shaking his head. "There's not a future."

"You sure about that?" There was no malice in Levi's voice, just calm acceptance.

"If things go well, it might be nice to bring Paisley out sometime. She'd love all this space after living near the city."

"You're not going to want to make the drive from Houston without a place of your own to stay. There are plenty of good spots on the land. You might want to think about a more permanent place here for the two of you. Of course, you're always welcome to stay at the main house," Levi locked gazes. "That is where Uncle Donny stays."

Kurt involuntarily shivered. "No, thank you."

Levi chuckled.

"Most of us have that response to him." He issued a sharp sigh. "Except we try not to show it around our cousins. Uncle Donny is their dad and we do our best to respect that."

"Sounds like a plan." His comment elicited a genuine smile from Levi.

"You're going to fit in better than you realize."

Kurt wasn't so sure about that. He did have questions mounting about their father—questions he'd like answers to. He tabled those thoughts as he hopped back into the driver's side as Levi grabbed a truck. He led the way around the impressive barns and past the baseball diamond. They were on a gravel road for a solid ten minutes before stopping in front of a one-story ranch-style cabin.

The place was surrounded by trees and beyond that was a rolling meadow. Strangely, the image that came to mind was Paisley running through bluebonnets in spring. So, yeah, he was rocking the whole *I don't want a place here* vibe.

He parked next to Levi.

"Looks like this going to be our home for the next few days at least," he said to Arianna, who'd been soaking it all in quietly.

"It's beautiful." Her voice washed over him and the kisses they'd shared burned into his memory. It was probably a good thing they wouldn't be alone in the cabin even though he was starting to wonder why it seemed like a good idea to fight the feelings growing between them.

Based on the outside of the cabin, it was already impressive. The place was one story and far from rustic. In fact, it looked like they only used the highest quality materials during construction.

Arianna moved around to the driver's side, suitcase in hand, as Kurt roused Paisley and let Cuzya out. She darted over to Levi, who was getting out of his truck. The two seemed to make fast friends. Since Cuzya was a good judge of character, her reaction to Levi went a long way toward building more trust.

The trio met with Levi and Cuzya on the covered porch that had two rockers. The place seemed built for two. So, this was going to be interesting.

"Levi, meet Arianna Ballard. She's a friend of mine."

Levi shook her extended hand as they exchanged greetings. He turned his attention to Paisley and said, "This must be my niece."

"That's right." More of that warmth spread through him at seeing how easily Levi accepted her.

Paisley's ear-to-ear grin was aimed at her uncle. Uncle. That was a word that would take some getting used to. There were a lot of *changes coming at him all at once without much time to process, and yet, Arianna, Levi, it all felt right.*

A perk to getting older was that it became easier and easier to identify what really mattered in life. It was also easier to see through a load of bull. He thought he was really good at that until Devin. That had him concerned. Were there signs that he'd missed? There had to have been. And he'd be kicking himself for a long time over the guilt that came with that revelation.

"Welcome. I hope you'll make yourselves at home. This is a three bedroom. I hope that it'll be enough space for you guys," Levi said.

"I'm sure it'll do the trick. We probably won't be staying here too long. Your hospitality is appreciated," Kurt reassured.

"Follow me." Levi pulled a set of keys out of his pocket and used one to unlock the door. Once inside, he held the keys out to Kurt, who took them.

The inside was just as impressive as the outside. The place was cozy and comfortable. There was a pair of large oversized leather sofas facing each other in the living room. A good-sized flat-screen TV was mounted above the fireplace.

The wood flooring had one of those plush-looking rugs in the living room with a coffee table that looked handmade. Kurt was grateful for the soft edges. The place could easily accommodate Paisley and looked to be baby-proofed with covers on the outlets. The kitchen and living room were open concept. A small dining room rounded out the main living space. Again, the table looked hand-carved. There were comfortable cloth chairs pushed around it. A massive granite island had more chairs. Stainless steel appliances rounded out the look.

"The master bedroom is down that hallway and the other two bedrooms join together through a bathroom. I wasn't sure which room you'd want the crib in, so I had that put in the master. It can easily be moved if that's not where you want it to go. They're all good-sized rooms. The master has an attached bathroom. The garage has a Jeep

inside, and you already have the keys to that. There are a couple of ATVs inside if you need those. Washroom is off to that end by the garage." Levi checked his watch. "I have a couple hours of work left. Better get out so I can finish running fences."

Kurt cocked his head to one side. He must've looked confused because Levi offered an explanation.

"Paperwork and running fences are the bane of every rancher's existence," Levi said on a chuckle. "We have to literally check all of our fences on a constant basis to make sure nothing has fallen down or been knocked down by a tree during high winds. It's how we keep our cattle in and safe when they're out grazing."

"Makes sense." Kurt had a lot of terminology to learn in his new family life. He wanted to be able to talk about, or at least understand, what was going on when he talked to his brothers and cousins.

"A.J. is picking up Ms. Calaway. I just got a text from him on the way over saying that he was at the hospital and everything was going well. They should be on their way soon," Levi said. "They should be here before supper. We can all meet up at the main house if you'd like. Family meals are important around here. Our mother passed away when we were younger and we were brought up by a wonderful woman by the name of Miss Penny, who has taken care of us and kept us on the straight and narrow ever since. She puts dinner on the table around five-thirty every day and everyone's welcome. It might be a good way to meet the others."

"Will you be there?" Kurt asked, realizing that it mattered to him. Levi was a lifeline to Kurt's new family.

"Me and my wife. We try to make as many family meals as we can. Even more so now with what's happening with Dad. His accident reminded us not to take each other for granted," he said. "And we have a dog." He looked at Cuzya. "You'll get to know Karma. He was a bomb sniffing dog. He's making progress on the whole getting to know people and other animals."

Kurt smiled.

"Miss Penny has a rule about dogs inside the house." Levi laughed. "We don't really follow it. There's always a bowl of water out in the kitchen."

Cuzya would fit right in.

Would Kurt?

"A few more things. I set you up with a laptop. Password is written down next to it. Wi-Fi can be spotty out here, but you should get some at this location," Levi continued.

"Thank you for everything. Your hospitality is appreciated and it's nice to get to know his kids." He referred to their father.

"You might regret saying that once you get to know the whole bunch," Levi joked.

Kurt laughed. It was lighter than he'd felt in a really long time. This had the feeling of new chapters opening and he liked that Arianna was there to share it with him.

"I'll be on my way. Like I said, coverage is spotty out here so if you call or text and don't hear from me right away, it's possible I'm in a dead zone. Fridge is stocked. Make yourselves at home." Levi started toward the door. He stopped and waved one more time before heading out.

Kurt walked over and locked the door behind him.

15

Arianna made her way to the fridge and opened the door. It was stocked with fresh fruit and vegetables. There was plenty of meat and enough drinks to hydrate a small football team. She opened the cupboards and they were filled to the brim, as well.

There were plenty of supplies for Paisley. They'd thought of everything. This would be a good place for her aunt to rest and recoup.

"I can't help but think how much Aunt Bea is going to love it here. I don't know if she ever told you, but this is kind of a dream come true for her. She's always talked about living on some land and having tons of animals all around," she said.

"I didn't know that about her. I've spent much of the past year playing catch up on life. That's going to change, though." He put Paisley in the little walker that was next to one of the leather sofas.

Levi had thought to have the place stocked with plenty of toys and kid paraphernalia. Paisley was happy as a lark when she was put in the little walker that had lots of little gadgets attached for her to play with.

"What do you think about the place?" she asked Kurt.

He walked over to her until he was standing almost toe-to-toe with her. She secured her hands on the counter behind her needing something to keep her balance. Being in Kurt's orbit made her knees weak and her stomach freefall, like she was base jumping.

"I could get used to this place." She took in a deep breath and that only ushered in his spicy, masculine scent. Probably wasn't the best of ideas, considering she was trying to keep some emotional distance between them. It was next to impossible while being in the same room with him let alone so close all she had to do was lean forward a little bit and press up to her tippy toes for her lips to be right where they felt like they belonged again. Home.

She reached up and put the flat of her palm in the middle of his chest. His heart beat against her fingertips, pounding as fast as hers. She couldn't qualify this as a bad decision because nothing about being with Kurt felt wrong.

Maybe a better way to put it was this was a dangerous situation, dangerous for her heart.

"Remind me again why this is a bad idea," Kurt said. His voice was low and gravely, and it traveled over her skin, leaving a trail of goose bumps in its wake.

"Because..." Thinking of a solid reason was getting more and more difficult. Pushing past the brain fog that settled over her mind when she was in his vicinity was next to impossible.

"This is temporary, for one. It's not meant to last. My aunt works for you and that could make things really awkward later." She was grasping at straws here, hoping to come up with a win. It was hard to convince him of something she was having trouble convincing herself of.

She wasn't able to sell herself on any of those excuses.

"Right. That." He closed a little bit more of the space between them. Their mouths were inches apart. "So, you're saying it would be a bad idea to do this." He pressed a soft kiss to her lips and that sent warmth spiraling through her. It also wasn't helping her heart rate. At this rate, she wouldn't need to get in any steps today.

He feathered kisses along her jawline, following down her neck to where her pulse pounded at the base of her throat.

"And this?" He feathered kisses down the V of her shirt.

His phone rang, breaking into the moment. It was just the interruption she needed to clear the fog that was Kurt out of her brain.

127

He took in a deep breath, stood to his full height, and took a step back. He fished his cell from his pocket.

"It's Officer Forth's number. I better take this." He took a couple more steps back until he was planted against the island.

She busied herself looking for something to make for lunch. Her stomach growled, reminding her that she'd skipped breakfast. While she was at it, she could pull together something for all of them. Paisley needed to eat and be put down for a nap in a while.

"Are you sure?" The sound in Kurt's voice caused her stomach to clench.

"No, I don't have any other known hangouts for him. He's been devoted to Carla and I thought his job. Why? What do you think that means?"

Kurt stood and listened, and she could almost feel the tension ratcheting up in every one of his muscles. He said a few uh-huhs into the phone before thanking Officer Forth for the heads up.

After ending the call, he looked up at her, "Carla doesn't know where Devin is. She's worried because he sent her a text telling her to go to a friend's house and stay until he sent word. He didn't come home last night."

Paisley stirred, working up to a cry. A glance at the clock said it was time to eat and probably time for her nap.

"I'm sorry. I can't believe your employee would do something so awful," she said to Kurt, who started pacing.

Tension radiated off him and she figured this wasn't the time for him to be around his daughter. She was convinced babies picked up on people's moods more than anyone realized.

"It's mind-blowing," he said, starting toward his daughter.

"I'll take care of her," Arianna interjected.

He locked gazes with her for one intense second. And then he seemed to catch her drift. "Thank you."

"Cuzya looks like she could use a stretch. Why don't you take her out for a run?" She nodded toward the dog.

Kurt issued a sharp breath. He raked his fingers through his dark mane. "That's probably a good idea. You'll be all right here with Paisley?"

"I got this. Don't worry," she said with a smile, urging him to get outside and get some fresh air.

He walked right over to her and kissed her. "Thank you. I'll be back soon."

"Take as long as you need. I've got Paisley. I'll feed her and put her down for a nap with me. It's no trouble." The only thing in trouble was Arianna's heart.

THE SOUND of gravel spewing underneath tires outside woke Arianna from her nap. She'd decided to lie down with Paisley in the master while Kurt went for a run.

Arianna had been dozing on and off. She stretched her arms out and sat up. The blinds were closed and the curtains were drawn, making it pitch-black inside the room despite it being the middle of the afternoon. Her first thought was Paisley, but there was no sign of her stirring.

She walked over to the baby monitor and clicked it on. The other monitor was in the kitchen with Kurt, who had said not to worry about turning it on unless she left the room.

The fact that he wanted to give her privacy was appreciated. It wasn't completely necessary considering she was clothed and in a room with a baby, but it was a sweet gesture.

Her lips still tingled from the earlier kisses and the desire she felt was a slow burn deep in her belly.

She tiptoed over to the crib, and confirmed the little girl was out. Stopping in the bathroom, she ran a brush through her hair before going outside to greet her aunt.

Walking out into the hallway, she glimpsed Kurt heading to the front door. He redirected his gaze to her and the warm smile that came over his face lit more of those little campfires inside her.

Everything in her wanted to be able to go there with him on an emotional level. Could she risk it? There wasn't much similar about him and her ex. Kurt knew his own mind and wasn't the type to make a decision on a whim. And she did know him on a deep level, where it counted. She knew what kind of person he was, honest and devoted. He had a lot at stake.

Kurt paused and waited for her as she made her way toward him. When he took her hand in his and then pulled her into his chest before feathering another kiss on her lips, those campfires turned into a blaze.

She should probably pull away or remind him what a bad idea this was. Instead, she did what she really wanted to do…pressed up to her tiptoes and kissed him right back.

Pulling back was difficult, but she managed as soon as she heard a car door slamming shut outside. Her heart skipped a few beats when she looked through the window to see her aunt had been helped out of the car.

Cuzya was already at the door, practically crying in anticipation. The driver, another one of Kurt's half-brothers, had similar features as Levi. She also saw that same resemblance in Kurt, but she somehow doubted he'd want her to point that out right now. Probably best to keep that little detail to herself as he adjusted to his new family.

He gave Aunt Bea his arm as Arianna charged out the screen door with Cuzya on her heels. Aunt Bea's eyes lit up when they locked onto

Arianna's. She got to her aunt as quickly as possible and brought her into a hug.

Cuzya ran a couple of excited laps around the group before investigating the half brother, who didn't seem to mind.

"It's so good to see you up and around. I've been so worried about you," Arianna said.

Aunt Bea's gaze shifted from Arianna to Kurt and back. A question danced behind her eyes and Arianna still couldn't figure out how the woman did it. Even if Arianna had tried to get away with anything while living with her aunt, which she didn't, it wouldn't have done any good.

The minute Arianna walked into the house, Aunt Bea could tell what kind of day she had without a spoken word between them. If Arianna had a test that day and it didn't go as well as she wanted it to there was no hiding it. Aunt Bea would bring her into a hug and tell her that she was sorry before Arianna even had a chance to open her mouth.

On the good days, she would go straight to the kitchen and start pulling ingredients out of the cabinet and fridge, ready to bake. There was always a point when she'd stop and ask, "What are we celebrating?"

As Arianna was mid-embrace, her aunt turned to her ear and whispered, "Tell me all about it later."

"How are you feeling?" Arianna tried to hide the fact she was blushing. She held onto her aunt a little too long to be too slick about it.

When she pulled back and scanned her aunt's face for any signs of pain as she put weight on her foot, Aunt Bea winked at her.

"This is a beautiful ranch," she said.

Kurt was next in line to wrap her in a hug. She beamed up at him and it warmed Arianna's heart to see the two people she cared most about getting along.

"My name is A.J." The man, who was almost equal in height to Kurt, offered a handshake.

Arianna took the offering and introduced herself.

"It's good to see you again, A.J.," Kurt said.

"I'm glad you're here," A.J. seemed to mean every word. He had the same sincere eyes as Levi.

"I can take it from here. You have a lot on your plate with ranch business." Kurt shifted Aunt Bea to his arm.

A.J. nodded with a smile. "Aunt Bea thinks a lot about you. You're going to be a good addition to this family. We can always use more good people."

Arianna saw something pass behind Kurt's eyes that she couldn't quite pinpoint. A mix of pride. Hope?

"If the others are like you and Levi, I'm looking forward to getting to know them better."

Without warning, A.J. stepped in and brought Kurt into a bear hug. "I'll leave you guys to it then."

With that, A.J. reclaimed the driver's seat and slowly backed away.

"Let's get you inside." Arianna took one side and Kurt took the other as Cuzya followed closely behind.

Two steps inside the door and Aunt Bea froze. "Whoa. This is just as beautiful on the inside as it is out there."

"Don't get too used to it, Ms. Calaway. Once our house is rebuilt, we'll be moving back in," Kurt teased.

Aunt Bea might be good at reading Arianna, but the reverse was also true.

"Speak for yourself. Paisley and I are going to stay right here," Aunt Bea teased back. She smiled a little too intensely and that meant she was covering her concern. "And I think it's high time you started calling me Aunt Bea." She winked at Kurt and Arianna's cheeks flamed.

Kurt seemed to realize that Aunt Bea hadn't been updated on the fire. His expression morphed to a serious tone as he brought her up to speed, reassuring her that everyone was safe and that she shouldn't worry.

"Are you hungry, Aunt Bea?" Arianna asked, trying to deflect attention from her and Kurt's budding relationship.

"A.J. stopped off on the way over. I hadn't had anything to eat since six a.m. breakfast and I was in the mood for a hamburger. I'd be happy if I could just find a place to rest my leg. I'm supposed to keep it elevated," she said. Seeing her up and around was a sight for sore eyes.

"Would you like to rest in bed, or do you want to be here on the couch?" Kurt asked.

"Lord, I've been in a bed longer than any human should have to be. The couch will be just fine. And if you have a remote, I wouldn't mind watching one of those home shows."

They helped Aunt Bea over to the one of the sofas. He propped up a few pillows so she could take care of her leg properly. He also brought out a few pillows from the bedroom to put behind her back, so she'd be more comfortable. The last thing he did was put a blanket over her.

"I could get used to this. You're spoiling me," Aunt Bea teased.

"You deserve it," Kurt quipped.

"Is Paisley sleeping?" Aunt Bea asked him.

Kurt confirmed that she was.

"I've missed that little angel," she said.

"She has missed you, too."

The sound of tires outside surprised Arianna as much as it seemed to Kurt. He mumbled something about it probably being one of his brothers.

"That would be Raul. He stopped off at my place to pick up a few things for me since I was told we would be here for a few days. A.J. said it was fine for him to drop off some items. I hope you don't mind *that I invited him to spend the night; I'd hate for him to make this drive just to turn around and go back home." Now it was Aunt Bea's turn to blush.*

Arianna shot her aunt a look that said they'd definitely be talking about this later.

16

"There are only three bedrooms in this house, but it's fine by me." Kurt didn't seem able to hide his shock any more than Arianna could. She was definitely not letting her aunt get away with dropping that bomb and thinking she could skirt an answer.

"I can take the couch," she offered, thinking it was good for her aunt to have a relationship even though the secrecy was killing her.

"Oh no, you don't. If anyone's sleeping on the couch, it's me," Kurt argued.

Rather than put up an argument, she figured they could negotiate later. He excused himself to help Raul and the minute that man was out of earshot Aunt Bea perked up.

"Is there anything you want to share?" Aunt Bea asked, wiggling her eyebrows.

"Um, no. How about you?" Arianna turned the tables.

"Why not? It's as plain as the nose on my face that he's attracted to you. Don't you find him handsome?" Aunt Bea asked.

"That's really not the problem," Arianna countered.

"Good. Because I'd have to recommend you get your eyes checked otherwise." She laughed at her own comment. "He's a lot more than a pretty face, Arianna. He's solid. Honorable. Not the kind of person who comes around very often in life."

Arianna took a seat on the floor next to her aunt. She picked at the plush carpet, figuring she didn't have a lot of time alone with her aunt before the guys came in. She also knew full well that she'd be getting the details about Raul very soon whether her aunt tried to dodge questions or not.

"Here's the thing." She didn't dare look up at her aunt right now. "I do…I have…we kissed."

Aunt Bea sucked in a breath that could've been heard in Louisiana.

"That's what is responsible for the different look I see on your face," she said.

"Probably. I've never felt like this toward anyone before. Ever. It's a lot and hitting fast. How do I know if he'll be around in six months or a year?"

"Oh, Arianna. I understand what the problem is now. But what makes you think he won't be?"

"Because relationships. They're probably pretty doomed from the start. Right? I mean most of the time you date it doesn't work out," she said by way of defense. It was a reasonable argument based on past experience.

"Kurt is not the same as other guys. He's different and I think you'd be making a mistake if you shortchange yourself on this one," Aunt Bea said.

"When my last relationship ended. I was okay. He was okay. You of all people know that he wasn't 'the one' for me. But Kurt…"

Aunt Bea was rocking her head in understanding.

"What are you really afraid of?" she asked.

"It's that catch twenty-two. I won't know if what we have can go the distance until I take the chance and get to know him better. But getting to know each other risks more than I can handle."

Aunt Bea made a tsk-tsk sound. "What makes you think that you don't know him?"

"We haven't even known each other forty-eight hours yet, for one," Arianna said.

"That's true. How long did you know your last boyfriend before you went out with him?" Aunt Bea asked.

"At least a year. Why?"

Aunt Bea didn't answer. She just looked at Arianna with that knowing look.

"Point taken. You don't really know a person until you go all-in and see what happens," Arianna said.

"I don't necessarily believe that. Sometimes, I think you know someone without spending a lot of time together. You know what's in here." She pointed to the center of her chest where her heart was. "It's not hard to figure a person out if you're really looking at their actions. It doesn't take long to know what their values are if you look at their lifestyle. Kurt is a single father who has his own company and prizes his little girl above all else. He cares about family. He's like family to me. Did you know those things after spending a little time with him?"

Arianna nodded.

"Then, the rest is just filling in the details like favorite color and whether he likes pizza over a hamburger. That's the less important stuff. I believe the heart knows when it has met its match. Did you have that feeling when you met him?"

Before Arianna could answer, the door opened, and two cheerful voices boomed inside the room.

"LOOK WHO I FOUND OUTSIDE," Kurt teased. He was grateful for his neighbor and it was pretty obvious that Raul wasn't there as a favor to his community. The man had eyes for Aunt Bea.

It was funny that something had been happening right before his eyes with Ms. C…Aunt Bea…and his neighbor. He'd been so caught up in the now that he'd missed it. He also laughed at the idea he'd picked up another relative by calling her aunt. Couldn't say it was a bad thing.

All those times when Aunt Bea took Paisley for a walk with Raul and his dog. All those times she'd said Raul's dog and Cuzya got along so well when she was really finding an excuse to be with Raul.

Well, the writing was on the wall now. There was no going back, and he was happy for her. She deserved to be happy and to have someone who wanted to take care of her for a change. And the two of them couldn't be any more adorable. Raul had kept Kurt out in the parking lot for a few minutes explaining that Bea was important to him and asking Kurt's permission to stay over.

Raul already knew that Bea, as he'd called her, had asked A.J. and Kurt, but Raul wanted to hear for himself that he had Kurt's blessing. It meant a lot to Kurt.

"Does anyone want anything to drink?" he asked as Arianna made eyes at him. Seemed like she'd put two-and-two together about her aunt's relationship.

"I can grab some water," Raul offered.

"Nah, I got it." Kurt stopped for one second and saw this makeshift family. It was nice. He had to admit that it wasn't awful to be surrounded by people who cared about him and his daughter.

"Kitchen is right there. Cupboard is right there. I haven't opened anything yet so I'm not really sure what's in here but whatever you want is probably easy to find," Kurt said as his cell buzzed on the granite island. "I better see who this is. Make yourself at home."

He excused himself and got over to his phone. The screen read: A.J.

"How can I help you?" Kurt asked, answering the call.

"It's Dad. We just got word that he opened his eyes. We're all heading over to the hospital and I wanted to call and personally invite you to join us."

"I'll be right there. On my way." Kurt didn't have to think much about that one. He ended the call before jamming the phone into the *front pocket of his jeans. Glancing around the room, he figured there were enough people to cover Paisley. Aunt Bea knew his daughter's schedule and Raul could be a real help. Then there was Arianna...*

He looked at her. "That was A.J. calling about our father. He opened his eyes. They want me to come. Will you guys be okay here without me?"

"Absolutely," Aunt Bea said. "Go. See your family. I'm barely on any medication and I have Raul here to help out with Paisley."

Raul was nodding.

Kurt and Arianna locked eyes at the same time she jumped to her feet.

"Want me to come with you?" she asked.

"I'd like that a lot." He figured Bea and Raul could handle anything that came up at the guest house. They had Cuzya and all the protection offered by McGannon security. This location was as secure as it got.

Kurt grabbed Arianna's hand, linking their fingers before heading for the door.

"I have my phone with me. I'm guessing Bea has hers," Raul said.

"That's a safe bet," Kurt said.

"She needs to rest, so I'm hoping to convince her to turn it off for a while."

"Good luck with that," Arianna pointed out as a small smile upturned the corners of her lips.

"I have your number." Kurt looked to Raul, got a nod. "If you need me, I can circle back around in a heartbeat."

Kurt and Arianna locked the door behind them before racing to the truck. He had to take it easy on the gravel road. There was no map, but he'd memorized the route back to the main house. By the time he passed the parking lot at the house, it was empty. Not surprising.

His heart was in his throat as they exited the property. His father...awake?

According to GPS, the hospital was half an hour away. Pedal to the metal, he pushed the truck's engine on the winding road.

On this stretch, there wasn't much traffic. This area was mostly McGannon property. He saw signs for a couple other ranchers along the route.

"Did A.J. say anything else about your dad's condition?" Arianna finally spoke.

"No. He only said that his eyes were open and everyone was gathering." He glanced over at her, taking his eyes off the road for a second.

"Look out," Arianna shouted as they rounded a corner.

He cut a hard right and landed in a ditch. Airbags deployed. He and Arianna were jerked forward before being tossed back. Powder burned.

Out of his peripheral, he saw a figure running toward them.

Devin.

17

K urt's first thought was protecting Arianna. He reached for

the door handle as Devin made it to the window. His employee started banging with both fists. Screaming and banging, but Kurt couldn't make out what Devin said.

"Are you okay?" he quickly asked Arianna.

"I'm good. Shaken up, but I'm okay," she reassured.

One on one, Kurt had no doubt he could take Devin out, but he had no idea what the man was packing, so he tried gunning the engine instead. The tires spun but the truck didn't move. He tried to reverse with the same outcome.

He couldn't get the truck to move. Meanwhile, Devin was becoming more and more agitated. His right hand disappeared behind his back and Kurt knew exactly what was about to happen.

"Get low and stay low," he instructed Arianna.

She ducked her head and curled up in the floorboard.

The first shot fired at point-blank range. The crack of the bullet splitting the air. Thankfully, the window didn't shatter but they didn't have much time before it would.

Arianna gasped and his adrenaline spiked. He needed to get them out of there before Devin fired again. The window's integrity had been compromised. Another shot or two and it would break.

They needed to climb out of the passenger side. Kurt risked a glance and caught Devin running back to his vehicle. As soon as Kurt saw the reverse light on Devin's vehicle, he knew exactly what he was going to do.

Not far off the road was a tree line. Trees would block Devin's shot. If they hurried, they could get there before he realized they were gone.

"We have to go. Now," he said to her.

Arianna climbed up and out. He followed, barely clearing the truck as it was hit. He linked their fingers and darted toward the trees. Arianna stumbled a couple of times, but she was able to keep pace.

By the time Devin seemed to realize they'd abandoned the vehicle, they'd made it to the trees. But this was no time to stop. He was shouting as another shot was fired.

They kept racing forward full throttle. It was then Kurt realized his cell was still in his pocket. His lungs were already clawing for air, but he kept up the sprint. He managed to dig out his phone, unlock it with his thumb and then voice direct it to call A.J. as Kurt darted in and out of trees in a zig-zag pattern.

Another crack of a bullet echoed. They ducked but kept running. Devin was on their tails and they couldn't afford to slow down.

A.J. answered on the first ring.

"Help. On the road. Someone is after us. The road was blocked. We're running. Help. His name is Devin…" before he could say much else, the distraction of trying to get a message across to A.J. caused him to knock his shoulder into a tree. The cell went flying out of his hand about the same time as a bullet pinged a tree in a spot two inches from Kurt's head.

He pushed forward despite the loss. He could only pray that A.J. heard him and got the message.

Darting in and out of trees, Kurt realized they were going to have a hard time keeping this pace up for much longer. Could they climb a tree? Could they get far enough away from Devin to hide?

There was a creek up ahead. He powered toward it. At this pace, he wasn't sure how long Arianna could hold up. She'd squeezed his hand a couple of times already and had almost lost her balance more than that and yet she kept pushing.

The only break came when the sound of footsteps stopped behind them. That was also eerie.

Kurt glanced around, looking for a place where they could hide and catch their breath. The trees were thick, but the ground was level here. All he needed was to stay away from Devin long enough for help to arrive.

A thought struck. Could they circle back? If they gave a wide enough berth, could they get back to the vehicles before Devin? There was a strong chance he'd left his keys inside his truck. Could they use his vehicle to escape?

Running deeper in the woods would probably be a mistake. It would be easy to get lost and they could spend days out there being hunted.

Almost out of breath, Kurt stopped and surveyed the area. Arianna immediately dropped to her knees and grabbed her side. His ached too, but he pushed that aside and scanned the trees, looking for Devin or any sign he was nearby.

It was possible that he'd gone back to the vehicles, figuring that's where Kurt would head. Or, maybe he feared someone would drive by and stop to render aid.

The only sound he could hear was the two of them breathing. He squatted down, keeping a low profile. He wished he hadn't lost his phone. That was critical. Not stopping to get it was a decision he regretted but then a couple of seconds delay could've given Devin the time he needed to catch up to them.

When their heart rates slowed enough for them to think about moving again, he thought about the need to be strategic. Neither spoke and the thought occurred to him that they had the best chance of survival if they split up. Not happening. He wouldn't risk letting Arianna out of his sight.

"We need to circle back." He spoke low and so quietly he shouldn't be able to be heard above the wind rustling the leaves overhead.

She nodded.

He leaned over and planted a kiss on her lips. Maybe it was for solidarity or strength. He didn't know. He just followed his instincts and did what his heart told him to do.

Scanning the area, there were no signs of movement. Didn't mean Devin wasn't somewhere behind a tree. He'd fired a few rounds but would have enough bullets left to take care of both of them.

Hopefully, A.J. hadn't gotten too far down the road. He'd left first for the hospital and Kurt could only hope the run inside the woods bought them enough time for him to circle back.

They hadn't run long enough to get too far from the trucks. He retraced their steps, slowly this time. When they got closer, he'd make a right turn and walk a wide half circle, so they didn't come out of the woods in the same spot they'd entered.

It was possible Devin got spooked and took off. It was also clear to Kurt that his employee had gotten involved in something risky. Rory had confronted Devin and threatened to blow the whistle if he didn't report the trafficking. A judge had been setup in the process. At the very least to lead law enforcement down the wrong path.

Devin's nervousness and the way he'd looked at Paisley the other morning made more and more sense as the picture emerged. For whatever reason, and Kurt may never know, Devin had gotten mixed up with someone bad. The guy had a juvenile record. He'd admitted to it from day one. It was possible someone from his past had forced him into a bad situation.

Devin was a decent person and Kurt couldn't believe that his employee would've turned on his own accord. Something had spurred this, and Devin was the only one who knew what it was. But he was digging a deeper hole for himself and it was impossible to have too much sympathy for a man firing bullets at Kurt and Arianna.

When the trees started thinning and Kurt could see more light ahead, he urged Arianna to crouch down low. It was possible that he could hide her in a tree. No way would he leave her vulnerable to anything else that could be lurking in the woods.

The tree idea was gaining steam. Besides, Devin wanted Kurt not her. Except that he realized she could identify Devin. Being with Kurt had put her at risk.

Crouching low, he listened for any signs of movement as he turned right. He wasn't close enough to see if the truck was still there.

Maybe he could wait it out until A.J. arrived. That hopeful thought lasted all of two seconds before a bullet whizzed past his ear and launched into the tree bark not three inches from his head.

Arianna ducked and he put his arm out to shield her. At least now he knew the direction the bullet came from. He turned his mouth toward her. "Stay right here."

Before she could argue, he darted toward the spot where the shot had been fired. Devin was athletic and fast, but so was Kurt. Clearly, Devin lacked patience. That bullet might just be his biggest downfall.

Kurt bolted toward the shooter. He weaved in and out of trees to block a clear shot but, make no mistake about it, he was coming for Devin.

His zig-zag strategy was working because every once in a while, he'd see the glint of metal or Devin's face peek around the trunk where he hid.

"You don't want to do this, Devin. Not with a baby on the way." He figured getting inside Devin's head might make him question his decision or hesitate before firing. It was worth a shot.

Out of frustration, Devin retreated. He'd run a few feet before ducking behind a tree. His fatal mistake came when he stopped and took aim.

He hesitated.

With a laser focus, Kurt bolted toward the man. "You want me? Go ahead. Shoot me. Take Paisley's only parent away from her."

He was drawing attention toward himself despite Devin's shocked expression. *Yeah, wait for it, buddy. You're about to get what you deserve.* He stared as he tilted his head to the side, clearly a little confused as to why Kurt was giving away his location.

Kurt stopped darting in between the trees. He stood with a clear view of Devin and that meant the man had a direct shot. *Yep, keep looking at me.*

A secret was about to dive into Devin like a bulldozer. And that's exactly how it must've felt when A.J. rammed into the guy.

A shot rang out as Devin was pummeled by the bigger man. The gun went flying out of Devin's hand.

A moment of panic happened. Kurt checked himself over to see if he'd been hit. Relief washed over him when he didn't see blood.

He'd seen his half-brother in his peripheral, gunning toward Devin with all his might. It had made Kurt do everything he could to draw Devin's attention on himself, covering for his half-brother. The tank that was A.J. dove on top of the guy. Devin was no match for a guy of A.J.'s size. He was on top of his target in a heartbeat.

"I can take over this one," Kurt said. His brother rolled off.

Kurt pinned Devin's arms to his sides and then flat out decked the guy. "Why?"

No response came. And then a look of apology crossed his features. His eyes teared up and his face screwed up in a pitiful look. "I didn't want to. They threatened Carla and the baby. Where is she?"

Kurt's fist was reared back, ready to go. But he couldn't deliver the blow when he saw the fear in Devin's eyes. "Who?"

"Carla."

"I don't know. Safe somewhere," Kurt supplied. "Scared. Afraid that you're not coming back. Why are you doing this?"

"The trafficking ring. They came to me and I tried to refuse. They were from my old neighborhood. That's how they knew me. I tried to do the right thing and turn them away. Then they threatened Carla and the baby, and I didn't know what to do. They said they had a judge in their pocket if anything went wrong with the operation. But then Rory found the container and he forced me to call the law."

"You tried to kill my family," Kurt ground out.

"Only scare. The fire was them, not me," Devin defended.

Kurt was way too angry to think about helping Devin at the moment. But if what he said was true, Kurt would do what he could to get his employee into a witness protection program if he was willing to testify.

A scream and a grunt broke into the conversation. Kurt turned to see his brother carrying Arianna toward him. There was blood. Had she been shot?

A swirl of activity descended on them. EMTs. A sheriff.

"There's a gun." Kurt pointed toward the general area. The sheriff retrieved it before handcuffing Devin, who was apologizing profusely.

He immediately went to Arianna and took her from A.J.

"It looked worse than it is," she promised. "I screamed when he picked me up because he accidentally touched it."

Kurt owed A.J. his life, not to mention Arianna's. He turned to his half-brother. "I can't thank you enough for what you did."

A.J. leaned against a tree, looking like he needed to catch his breath. "It's what we do for each other. Right? It's family and I'll always have your back because of it."

Those words hit home.

"Same here," he promised. "I never expected to have a family, but I'm looking forward to being your brother."

"I'll clean up the mess back here. You ride in the front of the ambulance and go with her to the hospital," A.J. said through gasps.

Arianna shook her head and locked gazes with Kurt. "We've been apart too long. I don't want to go anywhere you can't go."

He kissed her before asking A.J. if he could borrow his pickup. "We were on the way to the hospital anyway. I need to get her checked out."

"Not before I have a look," an EMT warned.

Kurt set her down and she peeled back her jeans on her right hip to show the EMT the damage. It didn't take long for him to patch her up, but he made her promise to stop by the hospital anyway.

"That's where we're headed," Kurt promised. He helped Arianna to the truck and inside where she scooted over next to him. He put his arm around her, one-handing the steering wheel. She leaned against him and he suddenly realized that he didn't want to be without her. So, he pulled onto the shoulder of the road to have the conversation that needed to happen.

"Did you mean what you said back there?" he asked.

"Every word."

"I want to be together for the long haul," he said, putting on his hazard blinkers.

She looked up at him with those big beautiful eyes, surprised.

"The thing about getting older is that it gets easier to know when you meet the right person. When you're young, you meet the same people over and over again, and don't realize it. But then suddenly, someone walks into your life and she's not like anything you've ever known before. I knew when I met you that you were different. You've had my heart from the minute we met. I know what I want and I'm not explaining it very well. But you're it for me. Life contains some crazy twists and turns. And loss. None of that pain would be worth it if we didn't grab happiness when it was right in front of us. You make me see light when I'm surrounded by darkness. I love you and I want to spend the rest of my life loving you. So, I'm asking if you'll be my partner. Will you be my wife?"

The last of the cement casing around his heart became ash when he looked into her eyes.

"I'm in love with you, Kurt. I was afraid of the power of that because I've never felt anything so strong before. And I was afraid that I would lose it, that I would lose you. Paisley has been in my heart *from the minute I met that little angel. She's special and I'd love to have a ringside seat to the rest of her life because I love her father with all my heart. I've never been more certain of anything. You are the great love of my life and losing you, not giving this a chance, would be a devastating loss. So, yes, I'll marry you."*

Kurt kissed his future bride, his light, his home.

18

"**I** don't know if the timing is right." Kurt stood at the door, holding Paisley in his arms. Normally, he'd rather walk through a field of rattlesnakes than step inside the hospital suite. Being in a hospital at all usually put him in a sour mood. Having his daughter in his arms and Arianna by his side changed that, changed him.

"You were invited," Arianna said. Her voice had a way of traveling over him, soothing him. "But, hey, things go south and the three of us are out of here like that." She snapped her fingers.

There wasn't a whole lot that made Kurt break out into a cold sweat. The thought of being in the same room with his biological father was one of them.

"What if the others blame me for the hoax?" One of Kurt's half-brothers had received a call from someone claiming to be from the hospital. The 'worker' had said their father was waking up. In truth, Devin had made the call to flush Kurt out and get him off ranch property. The move had backfired thanks to A.J.'s arrival on the scene.

"I don't think that's going to happen or we wouldn't be here," she said, placing her hand on his arm for reassurance.

Facing McGannons one at a time was easier. The low hum of chatter inside the suite gave him the impression he'd be walking into a pack.

Curiosity had led him to this same door a few weeks ago. He'd been a jerk. Would they be able to look past his actions? Would they be able to accept Paisley?

The door opened and, head down, one of his half-brothers nearly walked into him.

"Oh...hi," Arianna stammered. Was she nervous? She'd been playing the calm, collected one so far.

"My name is Declan," the guy said. His eyes were set and his expression stern until his gaze shifted to Paisley. His features softened as his mouth relaxed into a smile. "You must be my niece."

The little tyke beamed up at him and Kurt wondered if his daughter sensed something familiar about Declan. If she knew on a deep level that he was family.

"Her name is Paisley and I'm—"

"Kurt," Declan interrupted. "I remember. My brothers said you might be spending some time at the ranch."

"I thought it might be a good idea for my daughter," Kurt said.

"We all hope to make both..." He took a step back and glanced at Arianna. "All of your family feel welcome enough to consider building a house there."

Another peace offering?

"I appreciate the thought," Kurt said.

"You three are just as much a part of this family as any one of us." There was something behind Declan's eyes that didn't convince Kurt those words were a hundred percent true no matter how sincere the man tried to sound. The gesture was appreciated anyway.

"If you'll excuse me, I have work to do." Declan nodded in their direction.

"Nice to meet you," Arianna said.

"Same to you," he said to her. "There are quite a few people inside that room who are anxious to get to know you guys better. We can be a lot to handle all at once, but you won't find a better group of people."

Kurt thanked Declan again. His welcome meant a lot.

"Is he...awake?" Kurt asked.

Declan shook his head and there was a palpable sadness in his next words. "There's been no change." He stepped aside to allow entry.

Too late to turn back now, Kurt entered the suite. There was a sea of familiar faces, but it was Levi who stood up and greeted them first. A.J. was second, followed by names that would take a minute for Kurt to memorize. To say the family was big was a lot like saying Texas summers were hot. To be clear, they scorched.

Kurt had noticed that Uncle Donny wasn't in the room and there seemed to be less tension when he wasn't around. Everyone seemed more at ease, relaxed.

After greeting each family member, Kurt nodded toward the room, "Can we go inside?"

"Absolutely." Levi stepped aside.

Kurt thanked his half-brother and walked inside the room. The machines beeped in a steady, comforting rhythm. With Arianna beside him, he walked over to the bed.

"We haven't met yet," he started. "But my name is Kurt and, according to a DNA test, I'm your son."

He glanced toward Arianna and received a reassuring smile. Paisley blew spit bubbles into her fist and he couldn't help but think it must be nice to be so innocent, so blissfully unaware. He'd said it before and was reminded of the fact now, looking at the world through his daughter's eyes grounded him. Helped him forgive.

"This is your granddaughter, Paisley," Kurt continued, unsure if his father could hear a word being said.

"Did you see that?" Arianna's excitement stirred his heart. "His fingers. I'd swear they moved."

Was his dad waking up? Was he responding to Kurt's voice? A surprising tidal wave of warmth washed over him as he stepped a little closer and took his father's hand in his.

"It's okay. You rest now. I'm here and I'm not going anywhere. We're going to have a long time to get to know each other," Kurt reassured.

Those fingers moved again. And Kurt could've sworn his heart swelled inside his chest at the response.

DECLAN PALMED the keys to his vehicle as he reached the hospital parking lot, thinking how random life could be and how much it could change in a blink. He wasn't real sure about Kurt, his newfound brother. But Paisley. That head of curls almost had Declan thinking about a family of his own. Almost. But it would take a lot more than those round angelic cheeks and big eyes to convince him that locking in with one person was a good idea.

He took this as a sign that he needed to get out and socialize more. He loved the isolation of working the land but if he was looking at a random cute kid and thinking he might want one of his own, he was probably going a little crazy. Well, not probably...definitely. So, why did his heart pick that moment to squeeze?

TO CONTINUE READING Declan's story, click here.

COWBOY CONSPIRACY

BONUS - CHAPTER ONE

P iper Gold lifted her right hand to shield her eyes from the blazing hot Texas sun. She had no such protection from a grandmother on a mission.

"You might be pleasantly surprised if you stick around the house for a little while," Gran said with a tone that implied she was up to no good. The wink that came next solidified Piper's reasoning for heading back to the barn to keep working. She couldn't get too mad at the sweet woman who'd been the only female figure in Piper's life.

"Is that seriously the reason you called me over here? Because you have another 'winner' to fix me up with. I thought you actually needed help with something." She made air quotes with her fingers when she said the word, winner. She also shook her head and made a show of rolling her eyes.

"I do." Gran laughed. It was good to see her smile. Piper had no idea how much longer Gran's mind would be clear or even if she would still recognize Piper's face in twelve months. Tears welled in her eyes just thinking about the medical diagnosis that caused her to upend her life and move back to Cattle Cove to face Gran's future together. Piper ducked her head and coughed, trying to hide her emotions from Gran.

"Someone will be here soon, and I thought you might want to visit with him. For old time's sake," Gran said.

"I've got work to do." Piper shot a warning look at the woman who'd practically raised her, a woman she loved dearly. "And you

154

better not be trying to fix me up on another date with a random guy without telling me first. I've only been home four days and I'm here to spend time with you."

"No one is too busy for a gentleman caller." Gran's face broke into a wide smile as she filled the watering can, obviously pleased with herself. She shrugged, playing the innocent game.

"Gran. If I stick around here and chit-chat with a 'friend,' who will feed the horses or clean out their pens?" Right fist planted on her hip, she realized she was being a little dramatic. Piper was still reeling with how much of her life had just been flipped upside down and she hadn't had time to process all the changes. Because bad news always traveled in pairs, she'd learned that Gran's barn hand, Owen Dyer, had been called away to care for his aging mother in Fort Worth after she took a devastating fall.

Running Gran's business, COZI B&B, was supposed to be temporary until Owen could return, and then he called and quit. Hiring someone new was out of the question. Once Piper saw firsthand how bad her gran's memory was getting, she realized that she was going to be here for the long haul. Piper had volunteered to help out her gran in a heartbeat and would do it again tomorrow. She'd barely had time to unpack her suitcase and Gran was fixing her up with strangers. That part was a hard no.

Returning to the area where Piper had spent most of her childhood brought back a flood of memories. All of the good ones involved either Gran or her best friend, Declan McGannon. Gran had taken Piper in after her father was arrested and then convicted of a crime that he swore he didn't commit. She'd grown up close with Declan despite his popularity and the fact that he was part of one of the wealthiest cattle ranching families in Texas. She was quiet and kept to herself, which didn't help matters during her father's trial.

Declan was also the only one who stood by her side during her dad's arrest and trial. The two had been inseparable until her dad went to prison and Gran thought it best if Piper was homeschooled. Declan still came over as often as he was allowed between school, homework and his chores around the ranch his family owned. And then the two of them lost touch after her father was released and he moved them to Austin to get away from all the shameful stares and accusations. Being back also reminded her of all the folks who wouldn't be so happy to realize she was sticking around permanently. James Bowker would be the president of that club. She involuntarily shivered thinking about him. It was best to push those unpleasant thoughts out of her mind. Those were her father's demons.

The sun was high in the sky on a typical weekday in the fall in Texas, the temperature hovering in the low eighties…

"I'll be back as soon as the work's done," she said. Gran might be turning into a handful, but Piper loved the woman with every fiber of her being.

"Don't take too long." Gran hummed as she watered her ferns on the back porch, probably humming one of her favorite show tunes. She loved Broadway despite never leaving COZI B&B, the place she'd started with her husband thirty-five years ago.

"When you live in the best place on earth, why would you leave?" Gran's words wound through Piper's mind. Piper's grandfather had passed away before Piper could get to know him. From the stories, though, he was a great person.

In her teenage years, Piper had taken it upon herself to educate her gran on the reasons people took vacations. They were meant to recharge their batteries and try new experiences. But Gran wasn't having any of it. She'd wave her hand in the air and say that was crazy talk; everything she needed to 'experience' was right there in Cattle Cove.

It had taken years for Piper to realize Gran never left COZI because this was the place where she felt closest to the man she'd spent most of her life with—her husband.

Suddenly, the thought of losing Gran, too, struck like stray lightning on a sunny day, unexpected and dangerous. Physically, Gran was strong. Mentally, not so much. Gran chalked her issues up to becoming senile, but the doctor had confirmed there was more to it and now that Owen Dyer had to quit, it was up to Piper to help Gran live out the rest of her life in the place she loved.

Being in Cattle Cove, watching her once-fiery grandmother as she lost her mental sharpness nearly broke her heart. Since coming to COZI B&B to help Gran, Piper had been living equal parts frustration and pity. Her gran was the last living Gold after Piper's father lost his life last year.

She'd been home a few days and wasn't certain she was cut out for country life. She already missed living in Austin with its weird vibe and live music. The place was twenty-four-seven. Being back in Cattle Cove was a throwback. It was quiet unless she counted the crickets chirping—chirping that had kept her up all night the first night. Don't even get her started on how pitch black it was at COZI after dark.

The idea of Gran being forced off the property she loved if Piper didn't give up everything she knew caused a wrench to tighten in her stomach. She felt incredibly selfish feeling sorry for herself after the woman had helped Piper find her footing after her father had been arrested. Gran had also been there when Piper's father had died last year. Thinking about her gran's declining mental state added to Piper's funk. It was strange to think she would be the last Gold on her dad's side. Piper never really knew her mother. So, she had basically no relatives on that side. She'd played around with the idea of getting on one of those genealogy sites and tracing her family history. She wasn't sure she wanted to know. Piper's parents had been teenagers when she'd been born. All she knew about her mother was that the woman had handed over her newborn daughter and never looked back. Her father had offered to give over her mother's name, but Piper didn't really care. Her birth record had been sealed because she was supposed to be an adoption.

Piper's chest squeezed and her heart hurt thinking about losing the last of her family, especially Gran. Sucking in a breath, filling her lungs with much-needed oxygen, she grabbed the barn door handle and slid it open.

She loved the satisfaction of a day's work in the stables. She put her gloves back on and reclaimed the shovel she'd been using before Gran had interrupted, thinking how she needed to figure out a trip back to Austin in order to put her furniture in storage and close out her apartment. Her landlord, Briley Hope, had agreed to let Piper out of her lease after she got the call that Owen had taken off and most likely wouldn't be coming back anytime soon.

She understood the news about his own mother had come out of the blue and, of course, he should help his own family, but it didn't sit right that he'd abandoned Gran like he had. Piper was probably being overprotective but what happened to loyalty? Owen Dyer had worked for Gran the past ten years.

Piper still wasn't clear on the details of his mother's condition, only that he'd had to leave abruptly. Her heart went out to him. When she'd gotten the news about her father...

Rather than slide down that slippery slope, Piper dug the beveled end of the shovel into the pile of hay and walked it over to Rosie's stall before scattering it around. One of the best parts about being at COZI was the work. Sure, it could be backbreaking, but it was also exactly what Piper needed because work was good for grief.

After losing her father last year, she didn't want to think about Gran dying. It was impossible not to feel like everyone was leaving her.

She'd barely worked up a sweat when a loud noise startled her. She glanced around, realizing it came from somewhere behind the barn. She tried to place it but couldn't. Something faint and far off made the hairs on the back of her neck tingle. She listened for the unfamiliar sound, trying to figure it out. It wasn't a howling. It couldn't be a wolf, not this time of day. She thought about a coyote. And then she heard it again…

It made the hairs on her arms prickly. But what was it? And, more importantly, where was it coming from? Icy fingers gripped her spine at the sound. An animal? In trouble? Being attacked?

Pulse racing, she stalked over to the corner of the barn to retrieve the shotgun she'd placed there. The weapon was gone. She'd been forgetful lately with all the stress coming at her, but she was almost a hundred percent certain that she'd put her shotgun there. After being stalked by a coyote and coming close to being attacked when she lived here with Gran during middle school, she'd learned to keep a weapon handy.

This part of the country could be deadly. There were feral hogs in the area even though they didn't usually come this close to the house. She fisted her hands and planted them on her hips, staring at the wood beam where her gun should be. She issued a sharp sigh. Now she was the one losing it. Her shotgun must be in the main house. By the time she ran there and back, whatever animal was making that sound would be long gone and she'd be too late to help.

When the noise sounded this time, it was so loud and so gut wrenching that she took off toward it. She might not have a shotgun handy, but she picked up the shovel. She could use it to scare off whatever animal was attacking.

Frustration nipped as she bolted toward the sound. She supposed she had to get used to these kinds of noises.

Piper blasted out of the barn to the woods that weren't ten feet from the back door. The sounds, the wails were growing, and it was pitiful. Her heart wrenched. She heard something else too, but she was sure what it was. Something with a motor.

The animal cried out again—pain. The feral sound shot through the woods and blasted her in the chest. Whatever that animal was...

Wait, maybe there were poachers on the land. They never came this close to the B&B, but she couldn't rule them out and they were more dangerous than many wild animals.

Either way, she bolted toward the noise as she gasped for air. Running through the trees, she darted left and right, ducking branches as others slapped her in the face. The toe of her boot got caught in scrub brush and she faceplanted as the poor creature cried out in agony.

She wondered if those teenage Maddox twins had gotten loose again and thought it was a good idea to steal her boat and torture an animal. Because the other sound in the background was a boat motor.

The screams intensified. The howling intensified. The noises shot straight through her soul. She'd never heard anything that sounded so pitiful. Her only reaction was to keep running toward it.

Maybe she could scare off the attacker by yelling. She screamed, loud and wild, doing her best to be intimidating.

As she neared the lake, the sound suddenly stopped.

The trees thinned as she got closer to the water's edge. The scrub brush opened up a little more. A flock of birds flew out of the trees as she breached the line.

Her thighs burned and her lungs clawed for air as she searched for the animal, and it had to be an animal based on the sound. She white-knuckled the shovel and scanned the area for any signs of a wild hog or black bear. She'd heard they were in these parts. She saw nothing. She was one hundred percent certain this was where the noise came from, so it was confusing to get here and not be able to find it.

Was the animal dead? Had the carcass been dragged into the woods and she'd somehow missed it?

She skimmed the treetops and then dropped her gaze to the underbrush. More nothing. Her side ached from running. She bent forward and tried to catch her breath. She listened for any sounds, any whimpering, anything that could lead her to the animal. Her heart went out to it because those howls had been heartbreaking.

There was no engine-sound or boat on the lake. The water lapped up on the beach area, just like normal. There was nothing out of the ordinary. And that was just...strange.

Could she dare hope that she'd managed to scare off the attacker?

She walked around the water's edge, skimming the surface. She turned around and scanned the treetops again, searching for a predator. There was nothing. No one was around.

It was difficult to hear anything, even something subtle, as she sucked in bursts of air trying to fill her lungs with oxygen.

Piper stood there for a couple of frustrating minutes, searching everywhere and coming up empty. She didn't want to leave any stone left unturned considering a life was a stake. She had a soft spot for animals, preferring them to humans most of the time.

After a few more frustrating moments, she concluded that whatever happened out here was gone. It was quiet now, she'd caught her breath, and she'd already been walking around for several minutes. This was a bust. She said a silent protection prayer for the animal.

Turning around, she started back toward the barn. A few steps in, a hand reached up and caught her by the ankle.

Piper gasped and tried to jerk her leg away, but the grip was too tight. All she could do was scream. And she did just that. So loudly, in fact, the sound echoed through the trees.

AUTHOR'S NOTE

If you enjoyed this book, I'd be deeply grateful if you'd consider leaving a review on the book retailer/site of your choice. Reviews are so very important to authors (they mean so very much!) and they help other readers find our books.

If you'd like to keep up with new releases, and/or my general thoughts, you can find me on Facebook and my blog. You can also sign up for my newsletter at BarbHan.com.

ALSO BY BARB HAN

Cowboys of Cattle Cove

Cowboy Reckoning

Cowboy Cover-up

Cowboy Retribution

Cowboy Judgment

Cowboy Conspiracy

Cowboy Rescue

Cowboy Target

Cowboy Redemption

Cowboy Intrigue

Cowboy Ransom

Rescue Ridge

Stalked at Rescue Ridge

Targeted at Rescue Ridge

Murder at Rescue Ridge

Captive at Rescue Ridge

Mystery at Rescue Ridge

Crisis at Rescue Ridge

Redemption at Rescue Ridge

Don't Mess With Texas Cowboys

Texas Cowboy's Protection

Texas Cowboy Justice

Texas Cowboy's Honor

KEITH: Firebrand Cowboys

TRAVIS: Firebrand Cowboys

KELLAN: Firebrand Cowboys

For more of Barb's books, visit www.BarbHan.com.

ABOUT THE AUTHOR

Barb Han is a USA TODAY and Publisher's Weekly Bestselling Author. Reviewers have called her books "gripping" and "heartfelt."

Barb lives in Texas—her true north—with her adventurous family, a Scottish terrier/poodle mix, and a spunky rescue who is often referred to as a hot mess. She is the proud owner of too many books (if there is such a thing). When not writing, she can be found exploring new cities, on a mountain either hiking or skiing depending on the season, or swimming in her own backyard.

Sign up for Barb's newsletter at www.BarbHan.com.